BADGER CARIBOU ENTERPRISE

438   ~   CONNELLSVILLE   ~   15425

a   limited   liability   company

ANOTHER AMERICAN TRIANGLE
preservation edition

This is a work of fiction. Names, characters, places, and incidents either are the product of the author's imagination or are used fictitiously, and any resemblance to actual persons, living or dead, events, or locales is entirely coincidental.

ISBN-13: 978-0-9884435-1-8

<u>PRODUCTION HISTORY</u>
ANOTHER AMERICAN TRIANGLE : PRESERVATION EDITION
preserves the cover design and the interior design of the
1000 EACH $1000 HEIRLOOM edition
— Each Copy Handmade by the Author —
Hardcover 2013

produced by
BADGER CARIBOU ENTERPRISE
PO BOX 438
CONNELLSVILLE PA 15425

Grateful Acknowledgements

for epigraphs of artistic literary device to the following authors :

STEPHEN KING

UNKNOWN

WILLIAM SHAKESPEARE

FIONA APPLE

SAUL BELLOW

LAMONT DOZIER,
EDWARD HOLLAND JR,
&
BRIAN HOLLAND

BERNIE TAUPIN

JOE CARPENTER,
WAYNE COCHRAN,
RANDALL HOYAL,
&
BOBBY MCGLON

WILLIAM FAULKNER

SIMON NAPIER-BELL
&
VICKI WICKHAM

another

american   triangle

NOVEL

for my parents

ANOTHER AMERICAN TRIANGLE

<u>c o n t e n t s</u>

PROLOGUE

I.

'No man,' the driver said kindly. He touched the back of Andy's neck lightly. 'Life is short and pain is long and we were all put on this earth to help each other. The comic book philosophy of Jim Paulson in a nutshell. Take good care of the little stranger.'

FIRESTARTER, *stephen king*

As we are but of yesterday and have no knowledge, because our days on earth are but a shadow.

JOB 8 : 9, *unknown*

CHAPTER ONE

THE LAST DAY

i

On the last day of his life David Guy awoke as on any other. First his right foot and then his left touch the floor as he sits up in bed while fumbling for the alarm; stifling a yawn as he stumbles to the bathroom. His rituals are the same : he brushes his teeth with his electric toothbrush and whitening toothpaste; washes his face and then shaves before showering. After the shower, he whistles as he pulls on socks, pants, shirt, and tie. He thinks about the weather as he walks down stairs. Over breakfast, he asks Davey what he'll be learning in Kindergarten that day. He kisses his son goodbye, not knowing he will never do this again.

The crisp frigidness of the air instantly penetrates, and David smells snow in the air. The sky promises it, and then the radio in the car is all talk of the approaching storm. Most probably 24 inches of snow at the finish is the prediction. This news in no way worries him, and his commute to work is otherwise uneventful.

The early part of his day goes by rapidly for him at work. He barely has time to grab coffee between presentations. One for a corporate office he's designing;

another for a commercial property being cut-out by younger colleagues he's advising, and both go well. David has to cut his official 11a.m. coffee break short — which he always spends with his buddy Byron Jenson — in order to meet with another colleague for planning-stage discussions on a condo project they're designing together. It seems to him that he turns around and it's lunch time.

This day he returns home for lunch. It's his turn to take Sarah — a personable Saint Bernard — on her walk. He neglects to lock the French doors at the back of the house.

Sketching diligently with his office door shut, David's afternoon goes by as fast as his morning. Trying to catch up on what he thinks of as 'actual' work, he doesn't call home mid-afternoon per his usual custom, because blueprints, spatial calculations, material weights, and project notes are scattered across his desk and mind. He realizes that it's thirty minutes after the time he normally goes home only because Byron pops his head in.

Snow is falling as he drives home. The roads are not slick or treacherous, yet traffic is slower than normal. David normally returns home before dark, but, on this day, it is dark when he pulls in.

The house is a modest Victorian, painstakingly restored to its original splendor. He finds it slightly odd that lights are not visible inside.

<u>ii</u>

Inside the foyer with the smell of old wood to greet him as usual, he flips on the light and shouts, 'I'm home.' The hanging fixture that lights the foyer also illuminates the stairs to his left. They rise to the second floor. He looks into the living room, off to the right, and can see the shadow of a fichus tree swaying from heat blowing out of a vent, and, pausing inside the arched entryway leading in to the living room, he looks out the large bay window. Illuminated by the street lamps the falling snow is eerily beautiful from within the quiet house. Even the dog hasn't answered him, but she might be asleep, so David calls out for her. The only thing he hears is a creak from the second floor. After more than a hundred years the house is still settling, especially during windy storms.

A hall formed by the staircase and an interior wall, the latter shared by both the living and dining room, leads to the kitchen, and David turns on every light as he enters, ensuring that the dimmer dials are at their brightest. The fixtures in all of the other rooms are vintage 19TH century, but the kitchen has lighting recessed into the ceiling.

Of the four chairs one is pulled out, and he tosses his coat over the back of it as he walks around the table on his way to the sink. Grabbing a glass from a nearby cabinet, filling it from the tap, and then drinking it in nearly one gulp, he fills it again, studying the odd chair as he drinks more slowly.

If Davey had wanted to go somewhere and they had gone. And if they figured that he was arriving home at his usual time, which has to be the case since he hadn't called to say otherwise, well then, especially, they wouldn't have turned the lights on. The chair, though, does not at all jive with Mr. Clean and his obsessive compulsive ways of house. In fact, if they were to walk through the door right now, he would hear it about his coat being on the chair and not in the closet. Built into the side of the staircase.

iii

A violent wind rattles the loose things along the backside of the house, and David jumps. He instantly feels silly, but the rattle has sounded like someone tapping on the window above the sink directly behind him. He decides it's too quiet in the house all alone, and he heads for the television set in the living room. During renovation the wall originally dividing the kitchen from the dining room — to the right of the kitchen when entering from the hall — and also the wall dividing the dining room from the living room — were removed to give the interior of the house a greater sense of space. David navigates through the dining room by the light of the kitchen to the living room, where he turns on the lamp before turning on the TV. He tells from the voices discussing logistics of internet music downloads that it's on a cable news channel, and he switches it to a network for the local news just as the picture materializes on the screen. The evening news has yet to begin. Being more acutely aware of the current time, David Guy wants to call his family. To find out where they are.

He walks into the kitchen through the dining room.

Glancing over the gargantuan mahogany table through the windows, he sees the snow has not slowed in its descent. He decides that when he gets off of the phone he'll step outside of the French doors. They open onto a bricked veranda, beyond which is a fenced back lawn. He wants to give the veranda a precursory shovel so that Sarah won't track in much snow when she comes in from eventually going out.

The phone hangs in the kitchen near the entrance to the dining room. On a part of the wall still remaining that forms a corner with the wall that the hall door is on. The phone's cord is long enough so you can look down the hall at the front door, or through the dining room at the TV set in the living room.

David reaches for the phone. His hand is barely touching it when it rings. His heart stops beating for a second, and he feels absurd for being so on edge, laughing in spite of himself. The phone peals again. He snatches it up mid-ring, and its shrill continues for a moment with impossible resonation, like a scream in a movie that doesn't stop when the actor's mouth shuts.

His hello is low and gruff. It's not calm and sure, which is the way he wants it to be.

iv

'Hello.'

'Mr. Guy?'

David recognizes his attorney's voice and answers in the affirmative.

'This is Simon Curtis. Do you have a few minutes?'

David says that he does.

'Sorry to call at this time, but I just received a motion for transfer concerning Ms. Bachman. Those damn couriers, you know, they pop in at all hours. There's a question of undue duress —'

David interrupts to ask what type of duress, in comparison to his own, that any court could consider seriously.

'It's bull, David, I know, but her attorney is pleading for clemency. Claiming emotional duress. He's stretching; knows he doesn't have a chance. But, if he can get the decision overturned, then she's out. Failure at a true appeal would only land her in prison. Obviously he doesn't want that.'

'He just wants her free to try and kill somebody else.' David is uncharacteristically bitter.

'There is foundation here, but it won't stand. We should meet to discuss this before the hearing, which is Monday.'

David is silent for a moment before arranging to meet the day after next.

<u>V</u>

He hangs up the phone. His leg aches, reminding him why his ex-wife — Susan Bachman — is incarcerated:

The 'accident'. The day she accidentally hit him with her Explorer.

That was 8 months ago. Last year already that it had happened.

She'd been sentenced — after having been found guilty of attempted vehicular homicide and making terroristic threats — to the Shady Grove Mental

Wellness Institute.

David hates being alone as he is now because he has too much time to think, and he doesn't like what he thinks about. Short of wishing himself back in time to change the course that has led him to today, David simply wishes for the whole mess to be over. No matter how he deconstructs the past or analyzes it, questioning choices and at times even specific conversations, he always ends up where he begins; so the whole process is just a waste of time. The simple truth is that nothing in the past can be altered. No amount of thinking is going to change the fact that he has to go to court again for another hearing.

The wind blows again and David shivers, chilled somehow by the heard but unfelt gust. He thinks of his mother, who often made cocoa for them as children during such wintry weather. If ever there was a time for cocoa it is now, so David decides to make some, enough for everybody, because they're bound to be home soon.

BOOK ONE

II.

CHAPTER TWO

~FIVE YEARS EARLIER

<u>vi</u>

At the time they live in the one and only residence they'd purchased together as a couple, bought shortly after they had become pregnant. He hears Davey crying as he walks into the split-level house. By then both he and Susan are pros at predicting what the baby needs based on the sound of his cries — attention, food, or diaper change — but David has never heard him emit such an urgent cacophony. It's an incessant breathless wailing, high-pitched and somewhat musical, and it sounds nearly inhuman. It makes David cringe. In any circumstance it would be painful to hear, but he knows that it's *his* son making those piercing wordless pleas.

He shouts for Susan as he rushes down the stairs to the wailing, convinced that something horrible has happened to her. He's forgotten all about her when he reaches the crib; his baby's face is chafed from crying and colored a painful looking shade of pink. With blurred vision he picks Davey up, and the baby boy's screaming increases with accusatory vehemence.

His diaper is leaking. The mess runs down his legs

as David lifts him from the crib. David cleans him, powders him, and diapers him, thoroughly and quickly, and then wipes his face with a cool damp cloth. Buttoning Davey into a fresh one-piece his crying has nearly tapered off, and David notices that he can faintly hear the television from upstairs. Again he wonders about Susan; about something horrible having had happened to her. He holds Davey on his shoulder, rocking him the few minutes it takes him to fall asleep. The baby had not been hungry, but obviously exhausted from exertion and discomfort. Laying Davey down in the crib, David thinks that perhaps he's poised to overreact to whatever Susan's explanation will be.

No. Even if it was only a minute, then it was a minute too long. How could she allow her own baby to go on like that? Our baby! This is not acceptable. It will not happen again. I will not allow it. Not my child. No way.

Heading to the upstairs, he concentrates on the sound of the TV. With the baby taken care of; himself in purposeful motion, his imagination proposes horrors of future sight. At the landing just inside the front door he realizes how loud the TV is — blaring — and thinks he should have noticed its volume immediately when he entered the house. But all he had heard was Davey. Now, because of this, David knows he'll guilt himself to no end for thinking at first only to blame her.

A mass of voices from the TV rises together as David tops the stairs; the sound becomes deafening with a high caw and group laughter. David pauses to take a breath, and he shouts, 'Susan!' He turns and looks into the room, half expecting for her to not be there at all.

Not trapped beneath a fallen bureau she had

been attempting to move, not blue and purple from asphyxiating on a grape or a nut, and not lying in a puddle of her own blood, no, the image of Susan sitting calmly on the sofa shocks him. She's lounging with her ankles crossed on the coffee table and with a coffee mug within hands reach; tranquilly watching some woman have her hairstyle made over.

Susan looks the picture of normalcy sitting on the sofa beneath the exclusive print she had to have from Interior Design, which hangs between two sconces she ordered with it. She's still in her pajamas; her unkempt dark hair is pulled back with a Scruncii. Just as she was when he left that morning, which is not normal.

David had shouted her name loud enough for her to hear it over the television, and he stopped to stand obviously within her peripheral vision; yet she does not stir. She remains absolutely motionless like a zombie. Her dead but seeing eyes are transfixed to the screen.

He marches to in front of the television and slams the power button with his thumb. It blinks off as he's staring her down, standing directly in front of her between her and the TV. She remains oblivious; her expression fixed as though she's watching the television through him. He waits to see how long it takes her to look in to his eyes.

After a few seconds she does move. She picks up the remote control beside her on the sofa and turns the television back on. An intensely loud and high-pitched gaggle of voices pierces his ears, with all of them going on about how much better someone now looks. He halfway turns around to see that it's the woman who'd been having her hair redone.

She does look better.

This inane thought does nothing except to make him laugh (only on the inside — and later) at its irony. He takes with purpose the few steps to the wall behind the television, crouches to rip the plug out of the wall socket, and relishes the resulting silence. Standing up upon completion of this endeavor something hits the wall with great force to the side of his head. It's the remote control. Its impact with the wall has caused its battery cover to dislodge and the batteries to spring out of it.

<u>vii</u>

Susan knows that something has been wrong with her. Since she got home from the hospital with the baby, 10 weeks ago, more and more she's had the feeling of living only to serve. Never a moment of her own. Never a minute without worry.

Even the first morning — the first day — she was to be at home with him alone, but she couldn't get the bottle top unscrewed when he was hungry. She broke into hysterical sobs. Before 10 in the morning she'd called David back from work. Her ever patient, ever dutiful husband.

The glow about her when she was pregnant hadn't been embodied within the baby, because at his birth it had transferred from mother to father. David was completely at ease with the duties of fatherhood, and she assumed such instincts would naturally rear themselves within the mother as well. When they didn't (at least not to the extent that she imagined they would) a bereavement so extreme, yet basic, settled upon her.

How could she be lacking? She'd finally gotten the one thing she'd always wanted, but it seemed to be cause only for resentment. She found herself not only resenting David on a nearly daily basis, but also her baby. An unforgivable emotion for a mother to feel, yet she still felt it.

On this particular morning Susan woke feeling quite content with her life. She finally had a routine, and she finally began to ask herself how she would feel if David seemed to her to not love the baby. Two months and two weeks and Susan thought the progression of strangeness, which had rolled in like an impenetrable mist, was wafting away as imperceptibly as it had come.

Lounging on the sofa, habitually watching her shows, this is Susan's afternoon time, when she relaxes while Davey is napping. On a few evenings, when her resentments were progressing, she considered confiding in David. She did not, though. She knows what she would think if the situation were reversed and David came to her with confession of such resentment. Susan does not think on this — her inability to fully trust her husband — for long. She gets caught up in critiquing bride's maids' dresses and wedding day hairstyles and make up application. She doesn't even realize that she tears up and weeps through the last 10 minutes of the story. This particular bride is hoping to conceive that night, if not during her planned two week Honeymoon.

Susan's tears dry up fast when the next show begins, realizing that the overweight woman being chronicled, who's clueless in terms of her beauty potential, is about to get some help. This uplift quickly turns to frustration, however, because the baby begins to cry.

<u>viii</u>

As she turns up the TV, Susan thinks : *The little tyke is really wailing, but it won't hurt him to cry for ten minutes. Am I going to jump every time he says jump for the rest of his life? I don't think so.*

She hears the front door open. She knows that it is David. She hears the front door shut. She knows what he'll think.

He shouts, 'Susan!' She hears him run down the stairs. Davey's shrieks crescendo, so Susan turns up the TV some more. She decides to stick to her initial plan and watch the rest of her show.

Who does he think he is? He's not going to dictate to me!

She turns the TV up even more and hopes that he'll be busy with the baby until the show is over.

'Susan!' David shouts again and she realizes that he's at the top of the stairs.

I'm not going to move.

David turns off and stands in front of the TV.

Tyrannical. Oppressive. That's what this is. Stay calm, Susan. Just stay calm, girl.

Susan reaches over for the remote as calmly as she can and turns the TV back on.

I have to see how they fixed her. Why doesn't he get that?

David careens to glance at the screen. Susan peers at his hateful countenance before he gallops away from in front of the TV. Then she sees her, the woman whose makeover is now complete.

Look at that! Just the hair alone. And the make up! Five years younger at least. Good for her. I'm so happy for her. And that outfit. The blouse is perfect. I love that belt. The skirt is...

The screen goes black.

What the . . . ? He unplugged the television. I wanted to see her God damned shoes! That asshole ruins everything. Now hear it comes: Don't you love your son? Yes, David, but maybe not you. Right now I don't. I hate your fucking face! My husband is not my father. He had no right. David has no right.

Susan feels something in her hand. It is plastic, creaking from her tight grip. Blinded and guided by primordial rage, fueled by confusion, self doubt and guilt, it launches itself towards his head.

<u>ix</u>

They glare at each other. Each is contemplating their odds for the outcome of the battle.

David feels protected by the glass topped coffee table intersecting the few feet between them. Susan sits defiantly on the sofa. Her venomous gaze urges him to make a move or to speak.

Finally, she says, 'What, David, what?'

He looks at her uncomprehendingly. He hears deep tears in a voice that has anger all over its face.

She says, 'I can't stand the way you're looking at me. Just say it.'

'What in hell is the matter with you? Davey shrieking like a banshee and you're lounged out, TV so loud you don't hear him! *My* son, Susan, so tell me what the *fuck* you are thinking!'

'*Your* son? *I'm* his fucking mother! Do you think

that I don't *love* him? You think I'm a *bad* mom, don't you?'

'Anyone walking into the house a few moments ago would certainly think so!'

'How dare you say that! I clean him; I feed him, all day, every day. You think you love him more? Or better? Fuck you, David! I gave *birth* to him.'

'Explain it, then, Susan. Explain what I came home to!'

'Explain my ass. You don't know how I feel and you don't care! Babies cry, David. I think that's a fact of life you can understand. Babies cry. And ever since Davey was born you couldn't give two shits about me! It's all about the baby!'

'Then tell me how it's supposed to be! Susan! Susan! Is it all about you?!'

Susan looks down and away from David. Then, with rapid movement, her arm whips to grab her coffee mug as she stands up. She says, nearly spitting, 'Fuck you, David.' He flinches back a little when she stands, because he thinks she may throw the coffee mug at him. She raises it to the side of her head. It must be empty, because no coffee pours out of it.

Susan looks at David, and the expression on his face does something to her. Her other arm goes up as her fingers release their grip on the mug, and it dangles, hooked through the handle, by a single finger. She stands for a moment, forming the letter Y, before both arms flap to her sides. The coffee mug mutely bounces once on the carpet before coming to rest under the coffee table.

David asks, 'What is *wrong* with you?'

A hand goes to Susan's mouth, and her face is

struggling against itself to hold back emotion. Bursting a sob plunged from within her, she collapses into the sofa, as though falling buttocks-first through a hole, sobbing.

<u>X</u>

David watches her until he believes that she's being real, and then he sits down beside her. They shift eventually, he holding her as she cries on his shoulder.

CHAPTER THREE

THE NEXT DAY

<u>xi</u>

It is an ancient June. The rain hasn't stopped for three days : a veritable monsoon. She's on another binge. She started drinking before the rain came. He watches her stumble around the house, spilling drinks, burning things with cigarettes. He thinks it's a miracle she can function at all in such a stupor.

They've been fighting about her obvious alcoholism. She puts the same excuse to him for it. He doesn't defend himself. In fact, he says nothing.

'I can't stand to look at you, David. You're absolutely nothing to me now,' she says.

She stumbles to her coat and fumbles for it, and he knows she's intending to leave. He grabs the keys dangling from her inebriated fingers, Knowing she shouldn't drive, and determined this time to not let her leave as he always does. The confrontation takes place in front of the open door:

'How dare you! Give me my keys!'

He pleads with her with his eyes.

'Give them to me *right* now, David! Or I'll tell Mom. Don't think I won't.'

Thinking that one humiliation is enough, David hands the keys over to her. 'Please,' he says, 'don't go,' and he never forgets the look she gives him. This look is full of utter disappointment, utter disgust, utter hate.

His sister is gone. He hears the car squealing away. The thought that he should not have let her go, that she drank too much, is interrupted by a horrible sound.

<u>xii</u>

David bolts upright, waking to the shrill of his alarm clock. He sits on the edge of the bed for a few moments under the influence of his dream. He can barely remember the last time he dreamed any bit of it, and it's been forever since dreaming it so completely.

At least I woke before the worst part.

<u>xiii</u>

The rhythmic sounds of a shower are no relief to him, although the warm pressure of water on the back of his neck banishes the remnants of his dream. The gurgling of the drain, after it burps when he rinses out the shampoo, makes him think of Susan. Standing there, with his big toe next to the drain, watching the water cascade around his foot on its way into the black hole, David recalls the previous evening.

<u>xiv</u>

After awhile Susan stops crying, and she lifts her head from David's shoulder. He uses a thumb to wipe a tear from her cheek and kisses her. He asks, 'What's wrong, Susan?'

Susan pulls back from his touch, sniffling and wiping one of her eyes. She sniffles more and fidgets wisps of hair out of her face. She checks the bunch of hair at the back of her head and tightens it with her Scruncii. She settles for a moment, and then she says, while shaking her head, 'I don't know.'

David reaches out and touches her shoulder.

She looks at him. 'I've just been so tired,' she says.

'I know,' he says. 'Don't worry, Susan. Everything will be fine.'

She leans in, hesitating before she kisses him. She says, 'I hope so.'

'It will.' He takes her hand and stands up, so she stands up. He says, 'I have to make dinner. You should shower. Okay?'

She nods and heads to their bedroom. She showers quickly, and lets her hair hang loose to dry, wearing only a fresh bathrobe. She runs downstairs to get Davey into his carrier and carries him to the kitchen. She sets Davey in the carrier on the table, and while David finishes cooking dinner, she helps to set the table.

While she's filling their glasses with water, David asks, 'When is Davey's next doctor's appointment?'

'Huh? Oh. Next week. It's next Tuesday.' She pauses. 'No, it's next Wednesday.' She pauses again. 'Why?', she asks.

'Well,' says David, sautéing mushrooms, 'I want to

be with you. I mean, we should talk to the doctor together.'

She gets the glasses on the table and is heading for the napkins when she says, 'Oh. What are we talking to the doctor about?'

David stops cooking and looks at her. 'We'll talk about what was happening this afternoon, Susan.' He turns back to the stove after catching her eyes, continuing, 'I mean, I would assume that it's post partum, and, since you need to ask for help, I'm also assuming that you would want me to be there with you for support.'

David shuts the burners off and puts dinner onto their plates. He sets the plates on the table and smiles at Davey as he sits down. Susan is already sitting; she sat down with the salt and pepper shakers after placing the napkins.

'Don't you?', he asks her.

Susan is chewing and so looks at him. She swallows and says, 'Of course I do, David.'

<u>XV</u>

She takes another bite, playing with one of Davey's feet as she chews. When she lets go he gurgles and chirps, and Susan, exquisite, says, 'Oh, the baby likes his footsies played with, yes he does!'

Touched, David laughs, and he smiles so large a grin that his mouth is almost sore. Susan turns, smiling back at him, and he notices her bosom, realizing that she's wearing just a bathrobe.

'Oh,' she says, 'Mommy needs to eat.' As she

eats, David chatters about work, nearly giving a moment by moment account of his day.

They finish eating, and David cleans up while Susan feeds Davey. After, David says, 'Hopefully for the whole night, little man,' when they put him down to sleep.

<u>xvi</u>

Pat Sajak says, 'R, S, T, L, N, E. Give me three more consonants and a vowel.'

Barry, the contestant, says, 'Z, C, H.'

Pat says, 'Z!?'

Barry says, 'I'm feeling lucky, Pat.'

Pat Sajak laughs. He says, 'OK, Barry. And a vowel.'

'I.'

Six additional blocks light up, for a total of seven out of eight letters, and David thinks the word but doesn't say it until Vanna touches the lighted block revealing the Z : *Zucchini*.

'... seconds,' says Pat.

With the best mix of expectation and excitement, Barry the contestant says, 'ZUCCHINI!' The final block illuminates, and the studio audience roars.

'I'm going to bed.' David says this standing up from the couch. 'I'm exhausted.'

Susan smiles and says, 'Oh, really?' She sits up straighter on the couch, so that he has to look directly down at her face.

He smiles back at her. 'Yeah,' he says, 'and I have to get up early tomorrow. Long day at work, remember?'

She fake frowns. 'Yes, I remember.' Her smile is back when she says, 'He won the car.'

<u>xvii</u>

Susan watches television for an hour, but it's no fun without David. She shuts it off to sit in silence and think.

Davey fusses awake and gears himself into a good cry. Susan changes his diaper, sitting up with him a few hours until he again falls asleep. She shuts the lights off downstairs and then upstairs, stopping to check that the deadbolt is thrown on the front door on her way up. She heads to their bedroom.

David is lightly snoring as she enters the room. He's fallen asleep while reading something, she sees, because his bedside lamp is on. She can't discern if the open thing on his chest is a book or a magazine; too much of it is concealed by covers.

Susan walks through to the bathroom, and she notices that the light escaping into the bedroom isn't as harsh with David's lamp on. She leaves the door open while she cleans her teeth and brushes out her hair, not trying to be loud but also not trying to be quiet. She's hoping that David will wake up; at least enough to sleepily ask about something, like the time. He does not stir.

She pulls the bathroom door behind her as she reenters the bedroom, her grooming complete. Susan's grasp slips from the handle, and she silently curses her moisturizing cream as the door slams shut. David moans at the sound and shifts his position, discarding his reading material onto the floor. The magazine plummets with a flutter as it falls to the carpet.

Susan walks to her side of the bed. She takes off her robe and gets under the covers. Up on elbows, she shoves David's shoulder. 'David,' she says, 'shut your light off.'

He yawns again; this time with an almost understandable word or two. He finishes with a slow and sleepy mouth smack. Susan leans over him, her breasts pushing up against his back, and turns his lamp off.

David finally wakes a bit at her soft touch and the change of light. He musters just enough awareness to ask, 'What time is it?'

'Oh, you're awake,' she says, sliding down under the covers. 'It's just after 11.' She spoons up against him.

'Alright. Goodnight.' The two words are really like one and not really clear, but Susan makes the difference out. Within a minute she hears his light snores return.

<u>xviii</u>

David's big toe comes into focus with the silver edge of the drain, and he looks up so the shower hits him directly in the face. He opens his mouth to let the water in and swishes it around. He spits it out and reaches for the soap.

Lathering up his hands to wash his face, he remembers her front pressed up against his back the night before. He knew what she wanted but was too tired. He rinses his face free of soap and goes to lathering up his arm pits, and then his crotch, realizing that he's not too tired now.

<u>xix</u>

It took Susan a long time to fall asleep, but she wakes alert when David shuts his alarm off. She lays there listening to David enter the bathroom, realizing shortly after she hears the shower how badly she needs to urinate. Susan closes the door behind her as she enters the bathroom.

<u>xx</u>

Susan can't help but smile as she watches David's silhouette through the shower door while sitting on the toilet. When finished urinating, she stands up to open it.

The shower door rolls open and David starts, trying to get the soap off his hands as quickly as possible, while an embarrassed buffoonish grin replaces his shock. Susan stands naked before him. She glances at his erection and smiles lasciviously, but not without a bit of contempt.

David says, 'I was thinking about you.'

'I bet,' she says, stepping into the shower. She lowers herself down to one knee, directing David with a hand around his scrotum and the other one on a buttock, so the water isn't directly in her face. She teases with her tongue. His hands are soon on the back of her head. She stops when he thrusts too much, gagging her. She stands and they kiss, and then she turns around. She bends with her hands out to brace her, one up against the wall, the other over the track of the shower door.

The love they make is furious; the passion present is as potent as ever between the two. When finished they wash each other caressingly, comfortably sharing the shower. They kiss after turning the water off, before both reach for separate towels.

Chapter Four

THE FOLLOWING WEDNESDAY

<u>xxi</u>

David is in a hurry to get to work. He informed his managing supervisor that he'd be gone all morning, always erring on the side of caution when estimating time for an approved absence, so he's not rushing because he's late. Given that the appointment with the pediatrician was at 8, he figured on arriving at the office no later than 10:30. It's 10:45, and, traffic permitting, he's 10 minutes away. It's 11:05 when he steps out of the elevator onto his floor.

He has to walk past the break room on the way to his office, but David is putting a mental checklist in order. Someone calls out to him as he passes the break room.

'Hey, man, you just getting in?'

David pauses, registering only that someone has spoken to him. He turns around to see who, shifting the satchel to his other hand to glance again at his wristwatch.

A head is poking out from the break room to look at him. 'How'd it go, man?' It's Byron Jenson, and the rest of his body appears as he steps fully out into the

33

hall. He's sipping coffee. David smiles a bit and gives up on his rush, wondering why it didn't occur to him that he was arriving at break time.

'Yeah, I'm just walking in. I'm going to grab my mug. I'll be back.' In his office, he drops his satchel on the chair, grabs his mug from the desk, and notices the voicemail light blinking. Resisting a slight urge to check his messages, David returns to the break room. He gets coffee as he talks to Byron.

'So,' David says, 'the doctor said possibly post partum. Could just be exhaustion. He wouldn't say for sure, but referred us to a psychiatrist.'

'An actual psychiatrist? I thought everybody was a counselor or a therapist now.'

'Nope, Dr. Theresa Porterfield. My boy's doctor really went on about her. Like they're friends. He made it seem like a favor.'

'Don't tell me you've never heard of her, man?'

'Nope. Should I have?'

'I don't know, man, but that's definitely a favor.'

'Why is that?'

'There was just a front page article about her about a month ago. She's one of the most sought after marriage counselors in the state, but she has a general psychiatric practice.'

'I don't remember seeing that. What did she do?'

'What do you mean, *what did she do*?'

'I mean, what was the article about? It wasn't just a commercial, was it?'

'No, man, no. She's involved with the city arts program : the orchestra and theaters and museums. It was a bit of a bio about her, but it was really about cultural events in the city. Anyway, man, let me know what she's like after you meet her.'

David chuckles. 'We're not meeting for fun, Byron, but I'll let you know what I think of her.'

CHAPTER FIVE

THE PSYCHIATRIST

<u>xxii</u>

'Who do we have here?'

Dr. Theresa Porterfield peers at them with benevolent inquisitiveness. She's an older woman whose actual age to Susan is indiscriminate. Her expensively coiffed silver hair, her authoritative posture, her matter of fact tone, and her altruistic aura result in her exuding a natural tastefulness. David is instantly drawn to her, and, although her features are unremarkable, he finds her inextricably beautiful.

Dr. Porterfield continues by answering her own question : 'Mr. and Mrs. Guy. Do you mind if I call you David and Susan?'

David answers, 'No. Not at all, doc.'

Susan asks, 'Should we call you Theresa?'

The doctor sternly focuses on Susan. She says, 'No. Dr. Porterfield is appropriate.'

Susan rapidly blinks and moves a hand to cover an uncontrollable smile of disbelief. After recovering she says, 'Then I'd prefer it if you would call me Mrs. Guy.'

David shoots Susan a look he hopes will convey that she need not be so antagonistic. She notices his irritation but holds the doctor's gaze, knowing David will not interrupt their current exchange.

Dr. Porterfield, without pause or any visible sign of having taken offense, says, 'That's fine, Mrs. Guy. Trust is extremely important, and the more comfortable you are the better. In order for me to do my best to help you, both of you must be honest. Not only with me, but especially yourselves. Do you agree with that, Mrs. Guy?'

Susan doesn't expect the doctor to acquiesce so quickly and takes a moment to answer. She says with a smirk, 'I suppose.'

Dr. Porterfield picks up a fine looking pen and with a delicate, almost loving motion, takes off its cap and puts it on the end. She writes a few words on a pad already before her, and then she looks up at David. She asks him, 'Do you agree with it?'

'In this circumstance I do; yes,' he answers.

The doctor writes another word or two. It's hard for David to tell just how many, but it's not many. She says, 'Since this is our first meeting we'll spend the time getting acquainted, and I'll likely do most of the talking. Unless you have questions, which I enjoy answering. So if a question occurs to you as I speak don't hesitate to ask. Our dialogue must be clear in order for us to communicate the truth. I don't want to misinterpret what you say, and I don't want you to misinterpret what I say. I will often ask you to rephrase or further explain a statement if its meaning isn't clear to me, and my hope is that you will do the same for me. Do you understand?'

David and Susan nod like apt pupils.

The doctor jots something again on her pad, and then she continues: 'Everything we speak about is confidential. If and when I meet with you separately that still holds, which means that I'm not going to discuss one individual with the other. This is about you only, and when you're here together it's about how you relate to each other.'

Susan, having begun to fidget, says, 'We don't need marriage counseling. I don't even know why David is here.'

Dr. Porterfield quickly writes again on her pad. She says, 'As a psychiatrist, obviously, I'm biased, Mrs. Guy. I believe counseling to be extremely therapeutic and that anyone benefits from productive therapy, if only to achieve peace of mind. However, to adequately address those concerns I'll need more information. It may not be necessary for David to be involved, but, since you share your lives, don't you think the solution you desire is best sought by the two of you together?'

David is nodding as Susan says, 'I suppose, but wouldn't it be simpler for me to just take a pill or something?'

'I will evaluate the need for medication. That is one of the things I do for my patients, but, again, I'll need more information. So, Mrs. Guy, tell me what brings you and your husband here today?'

Susan sighs and shifts in her chair. She can feel David's eyes peering into the side of her face. She says, 'I promised David I would be a good sport about this, so forgive me for being a little suspicious about how effective it will be. I guess I don't understand how it could work. I'm not depressed. I'm just, well, I guess I haven't been as happy as he thinks I should be since Davey was born.'

Dr. Porterfield nods a few times before asking, 'Is

Davey your first child?' They both nod, and the doctor asks Susan, 'Would you say that you are only here for or because of David?'

Susan looks at David. She looks back at the doctor. She says, 'Yes, I would.'

Dr. Porterfield locks eyes with Susan and says, 'Thank you for being honest with me, Mrs. Guy.' She looks down to write something.

As the doctor is writing Susan looks down at her hands, over at David, and finally back at the Doctor. Susan says, 'Doctor Porterfield, if you prefer you can call me Susan.'

The doctor lays her pen down and clasps her fingers, leaning forward so her hands rest on the pad. 'I prefer you to be comfortable,' she says.

'Call me Susan.'

'Very well, I will from now on.' Dr. Porterfield assumes her previous posture and picks up her pen. 'David, what do you hope to accomplish here?'

David adjusts himself in his seat and then answers, 'I'm concerned about Susan. I want her to get back to her old self again.'

'You want her to be the way she was before the baby was born?'

'I think she should be happier. I've never been happier.'

Jotting something down the doctor asks, 'Do you think perhaps changes in your behavior are affecting her happiness?'

David thinks before answering. 'No. But I haven't changed.'

Dr. Porterfield says, 'Tell me about Davey.'

<u>xxiii</u>

The receptionist opens the door to Dr. Porterfield's office for Susan, and she notices just one chair sitting in front of the psychiatrist's small desk. When she was here the first time — last week with David — there had been, obviously, two chairs, and Susan had assumed that was always the configuration of the doctor's office. Susan takes her seat, watching Dr. Porterfield writing quickly on her pad, not looking up. Susan fidgets with her purse before setting it on the floor beside her chair, looking at Theresa who is still writing. As soon as Susan starts to daydream the doctor looks up.

'I'm sorry. I had to finish up these notes. How are you this morning, Susan?'

'Fine. I'm just fine. Davey's sitter ran late so I felt rushed getting over here.'

'I'm glad you're feeling fine.' Dr. Porterfield caps her pen and lays it beside the pad, and then she switches the pad for a folder, which she opens. The doctor starts to read through the documents in the folder, and Susan perks up enough to see that it's paperwork from the receptionist she and David had each filled out before their appointment last week.

Susan smiles, remembering what she had leaned over to whisper to David while they were filling the paperwork out: 'They always have you answer these questionnaires and no one reads them.'

The doctor finally looks up again and says, 'You indicated you've seen a psychiatrist before. Will you tell me about that, please?'

'I had a slight nervous breakdown towards the end of my freshman year of college. It was the stress and everything.'

'What's everything, Susan?'

Susan shifts in her seat, obviously becoming uncomfortable. She says, 'It's been so long since I've thought about it. All I remember now is that all the emotions I was feeling, along with the stress of keeping up with classes, it was like I couldn't shut my mind off.'

Dr. Porterfield nods and asks, 'What emotions?'

Susan's arms flinch up and she laughs slightly as she thinks. She says, 'Oh, I don't know. Anger, resentment, frustration. More than that I was feeling sorry for myself. Ineffectual and worthless.'

'Susan, do you know why you felt like that?'

'Yes, but, well... I've worked so hard to forget, and David does not know. It's been dealt with, so I don't really see why it matters now.'

The doctor leans forward to gaze more intently at Susan and says, 'Do you remember what I said last week about honesty? I was hoping the tests were over, Susan.'

Susan looks down at her fidgeting hands. Lowly she says, 'Yes, I trust you.'

'Then tell me about it.' The doctor closes the folder and moves it off to the side.

Susan takes a moment before she answers. She says, 'My father was an alcoholic. My mother divorced him when I was little, still in grade school, but the damage had been done.'

The doctor nods and then asks, 'What did he do to cause you to feel worthless?'

She looks down as she answers: 'He was extremely mentally abusive. Sometimes physical but only towards my mother.'

Dr. Porterfield asks, 'Will you be more specific?'

Susan says, 'No.'

The doctor picks up her pen and fluidly uncaps it without taking her eyes off of Susan. She writes on the pad, and then has Susan fill out release forms for prior medical records. They spend the remainder of the session discussing David, her relationship with him, and the changes she's noticed about him since the baby was born.

'I don't believe I would be able to be with any other man,' Susan says at one point, 'because of my father.' She wants to explain but can't find the right words to express her thoughts, words that will elucidate her feelings about David's manner; how he's not the testosterone overloaded typical *I'm in charge because I have the penis* sort of guy.

'Do you know why that is?'

'I don't feel threatened by David,' she finally answers. 'It's why I love him. It's probably why I was attracted to him in the first place.'

Towards the end of the hour Dr. Porterfield asks, 'What would you do if David left you, Susan?'

Visibly shaken by the question, it is obvious the thought has never occurred to her. Susan notices the doctor writing again as she answers, 'He'll never leave me.'

CHAPTER SIX

THE LAST DAY (2)

<u>xxiv</u>

As David shovels snow, though he tries not to, he remembers these things. He's finished the veranda in the back, and, as he begins shoveling the front walk and drive, he gives up and lets the memories come, beat by beat to the rhythm of each shovel full of snow he piles at the edge of the concrete.

It's stopped snowing, but he can tell only for a while. Six inches fell, only a quarter of what's expected before dawn. He breathes deeply the cold, dry air, in through his nose and out his mouth so his teeth won't feel frozen, like the memory of his solo sessions with the psychiatrist.

The wind gusts, and David leans over the shovel with his face away from the bitter breeze. The wind subsides, and he gauges with a glance that only a few feet of walk remains.

It's snowing again by the time he finishes shoveling the sidewalk. As he begins clearing the snow from the driveway, fat, wet flakes are seesawing, swinging like pendulum weights, and sometimes pogo sticking higher in their inevitable slow descent. The wind gusts more often, and he works quickly with his hood up and his head down, protecting his face from the freeze as best he can.

<u>XXV</u>

When he finishes clearing the snow from the driveway, finally, David is more in his past than his current surrounding. He still considers Dr. Porterfield fondly. He turns, heading to the back of the house, where he started.

His head automatically jerks up to one of the second story windows in response to peripheral vision. All the windows on the second floor are black except for the round one at the top of the stairs. It's emitting a soft glow from the chandelier in the foyer. All of the windows are just as they should be, but David surely feels that the light in Davey's room just went out.

A car goes by on the street behind him, and its headlights reflect from a window of an adjacent house off of Davey's bedroom window. The light is brighter in the thick atmosphere of the flurries, eerily diffracted by the snow, and David realizes what it was. Not paying attention because he was lost in thought, it must have been a trick of some random light. One of the street lamps, perhaps, or a car with bright headlights going by on the far street and the diffusive weather.

The cold doesn't permit him to think about it for long. The wind gusts are now a continuous attack, and he wants to get warm. Hurrying around to the back of the house he acknowledges that if his hood had been down he would know for sure.

<u>XXVI</u>

David props the shovel in a covered corner of the patio where it's safe from the wind. He thoroughly stomps the snow from his boots, which he sets outside the French doors. Three pairs of boots normally line up in this spot, but he noticed when he grabbed his to put them on earlier that the other two were gone. He knows they went to the park, but he's surprised they didn't return as he was shoveling the driveway. Stepping through the French doors into the dining room, he reminds himself to give them a call. David walks to the closet to hang up his coat.

BOOK TWO

III.

Hey, Romilayu, not even Death knows how many dead there are. He could never run a census. But these dead should go. They make us think of them. That is their immortality. In us. But my back is breaking. I'm loaded down. It isn't fair — what about the grun-tu-molani?

HENDERSON THE RAIN KING, *saul bellow*

Happiness you took from me
And left me alone with only memories.
Through the mirror of my mind,
through these tears that I'm crying,
reflects a hurt I can't control.

REFLECTIONS, *the supremes*

CHAPTER SEVEN

THE DAY HE BECAME MAN

<u>xxvii</u>

T. Helmway Architecture, founded in the mid-1970s by two cousins, Tobias and Theodore, and based in Columbus, Ohio, has built a national reputation, respected and sought after, that the two founders, both retired although they retain offices, are honestly — not just obligatorily — proud of. Still with heavy thumbs guiding the company, the two have sights on going international, which isn't bad at all considering thirty years ago they were a local upstart.

David Guy, still young and fresh, is one of their best architectural engineers. He's a non-boardroom employee : still sharpening pencils over blueprints in his office. Back in the pre-PC days he'd simply be considered an architect. His official in-house title, the firm's preferred lingo, is Senior Design Architect, and he's T. Helmway's second youngest. Many of David's supervisors agree that after nearly a decade with the company he remains the most promising, facilitating for his age his quick rise within company ranks. He knows when to push for unique visions when dealing with corporate contractors who have hired T. Helmway merely for the sake of the claim, only wanting a quick cut-out that keeps capital to a minimum. His name became known to the boardroom employees (Executive Architectural Design, officially) early in his second year with such a venture. Due to the client's lauding and subsequent word of mouth, his design of Akron's Buckeye Mall garnered T. Helmway acknowledgement across the entire Midwest.

The fact that David designed the mall in Akron also results in the consultation he has on this day. It's strange, and David knows it. He's meeting with attorneys, partners from the law firm Pructor and Lafete. Apparently Jonathon Lafete, originally from Akron, requested David when he contacted T. Helmway about some project.

It's unusual because typically only EAD personnel meet with clients at an initial consultation. David clairvoyantly feels this is the opportunity to ensure his continued rise, or the wall that will brick him into his current status forever.

<u>xxviii</u>

'What is it that makes you uncomfortable with your situation, David?' Dr. Porterfield waits for him to answer.

'I don't know. Aren't you supposed to tell me?'

'It's not my place to tell you what to think. That's not what I do.' She thinks for a moment. 'Most of my patients are well aware of their issues.'

'I'm here to help Susan,' he says.

The doctor patiently smiles. She says, 'Yes, you

are. Aren't you two sharing an issue, then?'

He smiles in return and says, 'Yes, but it's her issue. Not mine.'

Dr. Porterfield picks up her pen and poises to write. She says, 'David, I asked you a question, and you answered *parts of the situation make me uncomfortable*. What is it that makes you uncomfortable with your situation?'

He inhales and holds his breath for a few beats of his heart before answering. 'It's Susan. No, it's not Susan. Not exactly. See, I don't know!'

Her patient smile grows during David's mini-tantrum. When he smiles back, calm again, she writes something on the pad. She says, 'Does it have anything to do with Davey?'

Without a beat he answers, 'No. I love Davey. There's nothing I regret about having my son.'

<u>xxix</u>

'A jewelry store!' David can tell Susan is merely feigning interest, but the excitement to share his day, the details he can share, is too acute to reign in. He gushes, 'The Theodore Helmway was waiting outside the conference room. I'm sure Tobias would have been there, too, but he's in Mexico somewhere on vacation. Anyway, he spoke to me. I didn't think he even knew my name!'

Susan nods, listening while she sets the table. She says, 'We have to pay Davey's daycare tomorrow.'

David asks, 'Can't you wait until I'm finished telling you about this?' The words snap out rhetorical and sarcastic. It's not an honest question.

'You weren't finished?'

'No. There's more.'

Davey has been starting to fuss, and Susan picks him out of the carrier and hands him to David. 'Tell me in a minute after you change Davey's diaper,' she says. She looks at the pot simmering on the stove. 'Do I have to stir something or anything?'

Walking away with the baby, he says, 'No, it's fine.' David carries his son downstairs to change him, wondering along the way why she couldn't make herself be interested. It isn't that difficult to please him. Even if she didn't care at all, which he knows can't be because that would mean she doesn't care about him, it would be no effort to act as though she did.

Davey is squirming, wanting to touch at his father's face. David holds him away and speaks to him in confidential gibberish. He lays him down on the changing table across from his crib and starts to undress him, continuously talking to him. Davey sings gaga in baby glee.

Davey is still chittering as his father carries him back upstairs, but David has fallen silent. He's thinking about his day.

<u>XXX</u>

David enters the conference room. He's greeted by Martin Grimes and Elizabeth Cooper. Both are EAD; the former is his managing supervisor.

The large round oak conference table has two sets of chairs; there's a group of three and a group of two. All of the chairs are oak with plush dark sienna leather upholstery. Also in the room: in a corner a television on a wheeled stand with a VCR below on a shelf, and against the wall across from the door another oak table, smaller and rectangular, with glasses, mugs, a water pitcher, a carafe with coffee, another with hot water, tea bags, packets of sugar, and a small pitcher of milk as well as various flavored creamers upon it.

David pours coffee into his mug. Then, at Martin's behest, he sits in the center chair of the group of three.

Elizabeth walks back into the room from having stepped out to speak with Katy, one of the Executive Administrative Assistants, and takes the seat to David's left. 'They've arrived,' she says, more to Martin, who sits after he gets coffee.

Katy hurries into the conference room with another chair, struggling with its cumbersome nature. David begins to rise to aid her, but Martin places a hand on his forearm indicating that he should not.

Martin says, 'It's her job.'

Katy looks up as she gets the chair through the door. After situating the chair at the table, she says, 'They're on the elevator, and there's three of them.'

Martin leans onto the table to ask Elizabeth, 'One of the big men?'

Her expression says that she doesn't know but assumes it must be. She says, 'I hope that it's Jonathon.'

Martin says, 'I've never met either one.'

Elizabeth responds, 'Hope that it's Jonathon.'

Poorly attempting to not appear puzzled, David asks, 'Should I know who these people are?'

The woman guffaws and then subdues her surprise, smiling at David after with genuine delight. She says to Martin, 'This is what you get for keeping your subordinates in the dark, sir.'

Martin says to her, 'I thought he knew,' and then asks David, 'I thought you knew?'

He looks from Martin to Elizabeth, saying, 'All I know is I'm here because Martin... Mr. Grimes,' — Martin chuckles, because David hasn't called him Mr. Grimes since the day of his interview — 'said that Jonathon Lafete is from Akron and likes the mall.'

She explains, 'Pructor and Lafete represents T. Helmway. None of us know what's going on and everyone is curious. Believe me, the entire floor wants to be in this room with us.'

David realizes, because of her brief explanation, that she means the entire EAD team. Elizabeth lowers her voice to a near whisper during the explanation when three suited men step out of the elevator, even though it's anyway not possible for the men to hear her.

She says, 'It's Jonathon.'

Jonathon Lafete is in his 40s. There is an aura of youth about him at a distance, but up close his eyes are very old, the periwinkle irises hard and wise. To David, he's a carefree lad in dapper clothes.

Katy greets them as they step off the elevator and leads them to the conference room. She mentions the refreshment table before closing the door as she leaves. Following Elizabeth's lead, David and Martin stand for handshakes and quick introductions.

Jonathon says, 'It's a pleasure, Mr. Guy,' shaking David's hand. 'Quite a mall you built up there in Akron.'

'Thank you,' David says with a slight smile, 'but I only built it on paper, sir.'

Jonathon Lafete smiles back. He says,

'Remarkable design. I've known old Willy a long time. How'd you get him to go in for that?'

'I understood some feelings had been hurt in Akron concerning how the land was acquired... '

Martin interjects, as though speaking to himself, 'That's a diplomatic understatement.'

Jonathon Lafete nods at Martin. He says with curt agreement, almost conspiratorially, 'Lost investment. Loss of time; opportunity. More than just wounded pride.' He returns his attention back to David.

Feeling the need to comment on the interruption, David says, 'Battleground business.' Martin coughs into a fist, and Jonathon nods and smiles. 'Well,' continues David, 'Mr. Finke implied the building would make everyone forget, so I took that to mean he wanted a facade that would evoke local pride. Architecturally an easy challenge in a city with such a rich industrial past, especially once I conceived the food court rotunda. That allowed me to increase the size of the vendor spaces while still keeping the entire dimension of the mall within the guidelines.'

Lafete says, 'You're a sly pup, Mr. Guy.' He pulls his chair out to sit and says, 'Alright, let's get down to business. Marty...'

The lawyer sitting to Jonathon Lafete's left, also called Martin, sets and opens a briefcase on the table. He removes several folders, closes the briefcase, and sets it on the floor beside his chair.

Jonathon, looking at Elizabeth, says, 'We would like Mr. Guy to design a building for us.'

Elizabeth asks, 'Law offices?'

'No, no. That would entail a conflict of interest. This building is not for Pructor and Lafete. It's for one of our other clients.'

Martin Grimes says, 'But we're also your client. Isn't there still a conflict?'

Jonathon Lafete looks to the lawyer to his right, whose name David can't remember. He has a nasally voice with a small upturned nose.

'We can assure you there is no conflict. The legal considerations for Pructor and Lafete within this venture for both our clients, T. Helmway and the other, are indistinguishable.'

Elizabeth asks, 'Who's the client?'

Lafete beams for a moment. Then, with grave face and no sarcasm, he utters, 'The tricky part. Elmer.'

Elmer Dean. David suddenly remembers the lawyer's name.

In his nasally monotone Elmer Dean says, 'Our client wishes to remain anonymous. Further, all the details of the venture, from land acquisition to design and construction, will be need to know only. Our client wants no publicity. If T. Helmway agrees to enter into contract with our client for this project, then your involvement will likewise remain confidential.' He slides one of the folders over to Elizabeth, David, and Martin Grimes. He says, 'Adhering to our client's wishes we are unable to discuss further details unless T. Helmway signs a non-disclosure agreement and commits to the project in toto as a silent partner.'

Elizabeth's head cocks to the side in consternation. Martin's jaw goes slack, dropping wide. David remains motionless. Jonathon Lafete watches their reactions with obvious amusement, while to either side of him Marty and Elmer are posed gargoyles, looking like vultures ready to swoop in for the feast.

Martin Grimes regains voluntary control of his mandible and says, 'That's unheard of ...'

Elizabeth puts up her right hand, in front of David's face, to silence Martin. After a moment of further thought she says, 'Non-disclosure is unusual but not unheard of, however ...' She directs the finish of her statement directly to Jonathon : 'You expect us, T. Helmway, to commit without hearing a single actual detail and as partnered in the project? We don't do that. We can't do that. We implicitly trust Pructor and Lafete, but obviously we can't enter into any venture without being fully apprised of the financial ramifications.'

With his every exterior detail being reassurance, including the tone of his voice, Jonathon Lafete says, 'That's why I am here. It is also why David Guy is here.' He pauses. 'Remember that we are Pructor and Lafete. Remember that you are also our client. Ethically and legally, through years of both friendship and loyalty, we stand with you. Any disservice to T. Helmway would be a disservice to Pructor and Lafete.'

Jonathon Lafete pauses again. He continues and says, 'But, contingent with the demands of our other client we must stress this aspect of discretion. The particulars must not be discussed with anyone, not even colleagues. That includes Teddy and Toby. Elizabeth, Martin, if they pressure you for information about this project, you tell them to call me.'

He smiles directly at David. 'Trust me, this is a... an opportunity.'

xxxi

Jonathon Lafete hadn't said it, but David had heard it. The cliché capital G capital O *Golden Opportunity*. If the words were true, then it would be an opportunity for David, as for any architect in an environment where ingenuity was often suppressed in the interest of secured profit.

David gets back to the kitchen and places Davey in his carrier. The baby is still alert, his arms swinging, directing an invisible choir as he gaily sings along. Susan fills the glasses with water, and David plates their dinner. They eat, interacting with Davey as they do.

'I had an interesting hour at Dr. Porterfield's this morning,' David says, halfway through dinner.

Susan does not really respond. She emits an introspective mm-hmm concurrent with another forkful of food, but she makes no eye contact with her husband. This is either indicative of her wish for him to continue or that the food tastes good. Being elusive, she is focused, and looks straight out over her plate, down at her food, or at the baby with a smile. She purposely avoids David's preemptive gaze.

xxxii

The psychiatrist notes the resentment that emerged in David's voice. She jots on her pad without looking away from him.

'David,' she says, 'you have nothing to feel guilty about. If you've been having regrets it's typical. People think about decisions they've made in the past, and it's healthy to occasionally ponder what if? These types of thoughts are only dangerous when they prevent you from moving forward.'

David is nodding. 'I understand,' he says, 'but I don't regret anything. And I don't know why I said I felt uncomfortable, because I didn't mean it.'

Dr. Porterfield's voice becomes, in a way, motherly. 'David, you said it, and you meant it when you said it.'

Exasperated and loud, David says, 'You're making too big a deal out of that statement, Doctor.'

Theresa Porterfield frowns.

David says, 'I'm sorry. I know you're trying to help.'

'You don't have to apologize, David,' she says and sighs. 'Our time is up.'

David stands and walks to the door, wrapping a hand around the handle.

'I want you to think about what you said.'

He turns and looks at her.

'Search yourself, David.'

He rushes out of her office and through the waiting room, but before he can get outside the receptionist calls to him.

'Hey! Are you keeping the same appointment next week?'

David walks over to her. 'I'm sorry, I would have walked out and forgotten. Yes, next week the same day and time isn't a problem.'

'Alright, I'll see you then.' She looks down and David turns to leave, but she says, 'by the way, where's your wife been?'

David turns back. 'What do you mean? She was here yesterday.'

Shaking her head the receptionist says, 'No, she didn't come, and she didn't call to cancel. She missed her appointment last week, too.'

'Really?'

She laughs. 'Yes, really. I always get it when patients don't show without cancelling.' Her smile is flirtatious.

David turns and leaves without responding.

<u>xxxiii</u>

There's an officious little prick of a knock on the door, and everything seems to stop. Katy enters the conference room quickly, with apologies, and hands a folded note to Elizabeth. She exits just as quickly, shutting the door.

Elizabeth flips open the small piece of paper, ejaculates an astonished short sound, and hands the note to Martin. She says to Jonathon Lafete, 'T. Helmway accepts the conditions. We're privileged to be chosen for this project.'

Martin opens the note and holds it so David can read as well:

> *Dearest Coop,*
> *Toby called last night to say that E.P. called him. I'm sure you know they're close. He wanted me to remind you that we have a special relationship with P and L. They've done us many favors over the years.*
>
> > *Best Regards,*
> > *Teddy*

Jonathon Lafete, grandly smiling, says, 'Let's

begin, shall we?'

<u>xxxiv</u>

'Susan, did you hear me?' David thinks she's totally tuned out, but then she looks at him.

'What? No. I was thinking.'

'I said I had an interesting hour with Dr. Porterfield today.'

As though nothing prior had just been said, Susan says, 'Miriam Jenson started back to work today. Part-time. They have me training her; not that she needs it. Just a re-familiarization, really.'

David confoundedly looks at her.

'Why didn't you tell me?' she asks. 'Byron had to have told you.'

David looks down at his food, moving his fork around in it and trying to organize another bite. 'He didn't though,' he says, 'but I didn't see him all day.'

'You didn't?'

'No, I didn't.'

The baby coos and makes as though he's announcing something important, an obvious statement of fact to those listening in ignorance around him. He goes on for nearly a minute in a serious tone, seemingly speaking an unknown language, so that David and Susan both erupt with laughter. Davey has their complete attention for the rest of the meal.

They clean the kitchen and move into the living room. Susan gives the baby a bottle while David watches his game show, and they compete with each other. He's best at Before and After: A ROSE CALLED

59

AMERICAN BEAUTY IS ONLY SKIN DEEP.

The baby fed, Susan sets him into his automatic swing as a sitcom starts. David's attention, however, is on lies.

Susan sits next to him on the couch, leaning against him, and his arm goes over her shoulders. Her hand upon his knee begins to creep up the inside of his thigh, enticingly massaging on its way.

Her hand gets closer to something that sets him off, and, with an instant anger, David takes her hand away and suddenly stands. He adjusts himself to obscure his partial erection, watching the reaction on his wife's face to his abrupt denial of her advance.

'I know you've missed your appointments with Porterfield. Why?' he demands. 'Why make me think you went to them?'

Her face is blank, shocked, her eyes wide. The look angers him more.

'Susan tell me why!'

Her mouth opens, and it closes. A hand goes to her face. Unwillingly, she begins to cry. Fighting it at first, but then giving up, she hitches in a deep breath. 'I can explain,' belts out of her.

The lights — all the electricity in the house — goes out.

Susan stands up, saying, 'Oh, my God,' and takes a backward step.

<u>XXXV</u>

Elmer Dean does all the talking. They go over and sign the confidentiality agreement. The project contract is a typical agreement between T. Helmway and non-disclosed client, although via Pructor and Lafete; also, as with every T. Helmway enterprise, between the architecture firm and the law firm, for its legal services. Absorbing the intricacies as well he can, David puts his signature wherever indicated.

Once the documents are collected and necessary copies retained, Jonathon Lafete asks, 'Any questions?'

A perplexed Elizabeth Cooper does not hesitate: 'What is T. Helmway's required investment?'

The attorney named Martin, speaking for the first time since introducing himself, clears his throat and sits forward in preparation. He says, 'Two things. One: All fees and payments that would normally be submitted to you by our client will be applied to land acquisition and then to construction materials...'

Interrupted by Martin Grimes, who, bursting with a dynamic vigor, shouts, 'The land hasn't been purchased!?'

Everyone looks at him in reaction, but all remain silent. David looks to an embarrassed Elizabeth. Noticing her expression, Martin Grimes shuts his mouth.

Attorney Marty, nearly ignoring the interruption, says, 'Two is David Guy.'

Elizabeth and Martin both swivel their heads to David's, sitting between them. He feels as though an unseen spotlight above him has been turned on.

Marty the lawyer concludes, 'There will be no creative restrictions and few economic ones. We'll cover our client's desired essence for the structure momentarily.'

David becomes excited; is too excited to suppress a wide grin. Martin Grimes likewise finds it difficult to hide his reaction, and he scowls.

Looking directly at him, Jonathan Lafete says, 'No, Mr. Grimes, the land is not yet acquired, but it's in the works.'

A biting Martin Grimes asks, 'How long until it's purchased?'

The other Martin answers him. 'Technically that's not your concern,' he says, and David sees a smirk show through his stone face.

The silence that follows, emanating from Martin Grimes and Elizabeth, makes David uncomfortable.

Jonathon Lafete breaks it. 'We are, however, sensitive to your interests at this point. We hope to attain the lot by the end of the year.'

'The end of the year?! It's March!' exclaims Martin Grimes. He flashes a glance at David and then continues. 'Is there any estimate then for completion of construction phase?'

'Five years,' answers Martin the lawyer.

'Five years!' He looks to Elizabeth. 'Did you hear that, Elizabeth? Five years!'

'Martin,' says a flustered Elizabeth, 'there's no need to get so excited. As investors T. Helmway will earn in the end.' She looks to the three attorneys. 'Martin is a money man.' With levity she asks, 'What will our turn around be?'

Again Martin the attorney answers. He says, 'T. Helmway will be adequately compensated for its services.'

Elizabeth focuses on him. No longer flustered, David only sees the whites of her eyes as she addresses the other Martin. 'Gentlemen,' she says, 'T. Helmway doesn't want to appear unappreciative, especially because we do have such trust and history with Pructor and Lafete. Now, even though I comprehend the non-disclosure agreement, some assurances will have to be made. Given the extended timeframe of the project, Martin and I need something for our peers in the boardroom.'

Jonathon Lafete has leaned back in his chair. He has his left arm across his chest and his right hand at his chin, with a finger over his lips. He contemplates for seconds.

Nodding, he says, 'At the very least everything you normally would, just all at the end. We're seeking more on your behalf. You are our client, after all. We expect to come to an agreement soon.'

'How soon is soon?' Martin Grimes has a calmer tone, but it's still petulant.

Jonathon Lafete, correcting his posture, says, 'As soon as we know, you will know.'

Mostly to Elizabeth, Martin Grimes says, 'T. Helmway should specify the repayment of our investment. Why is this mystery client controlling all the purse strings?'

<u>xxxvi</u>

Susan trips over the foot of the coffee table in the dark. She screams as she falls.

David hears a bump, and under her scream he hears the clang of something striking the glass top of the coffee table. He feels the shake when she beats the floor with a low thump. She stops screaming, and then she makes an inarticulate sound.

'Are you hurt? . . . Susan!' David goes to his knees and feels forward. His hands quickly find her head and brush over her face. 'Susan!'

The baby erupts. His bawling is not unlike an ambulance siren.

Susan's hand finds David's, and he helps her to sit up after she says, 'I'll be okay.'

David stands and then helps Susan to her feet. 'Can you get him?' he asks. 'I'll be in the garage.'

'I can't see, David.'

'Hold on.' He retrieves, as quickly as he can, a flashlight from the kitchen, remembering along the way an obscure moment from his childhood. He and his sister squeezed into either side of their grandmother, listening to her hum, while their grandfather retrieved candles and hurricane lamps with wicks that dangled into oil. With the flashlight he returns to Susan very quickly.

'Here,' he says, handing it to her. She goes to the baby, having set the flashlight on the coffee table shining in his direction. David, once out of the limited visibility of the flashlight, navigates with his hands out in front and shuffling footsteps, making his way to the breaker box in the garage.

Thinking that he'll be able to see by light from the streetlamps, he feels stupid after he pushes the button to open the garage door, because he doesn't at first understand why it doesn't go up. He walks outside through the side door, and the twinkling light of stars is the only light to see. He hears many distant voices and sees their moving shadows. David leans back into the garage, his sight slowly adjusting, and from a shelf grabs a large heavy flashlight powered with a hunky rectangular battery. It has a large button covered with a rubber bulb meant to be pushed with a thumb while your fingers hold the attached handle.

Back outside of the garage various other lights are coming on, headlights and more flashlights, but down either side of the street the houses and streetlamps are off. The entire block is dead of power.

David walks to the end of his short driveway where three people stand. They're his neighbors, all with bewildered but keen expressions.

'What's going on?' and 'What happened?' are heard clearly, but otherwise greetings are ignored. Everyone knows everyone, or at least what they look like and where they live. In a sort of hush out of respect for the unknown, David's group of four is joined by a group of two. Across the street other neighbors are walking. Couples become triads that become quartets, and larger groups form that inevitably fission.

'A crash . . .'

'. . . snapped the pole in half.'

'Down at the intersection with Maple . . .'

'. . . driving a minivan?'

'No, a truck.'

'. . . said it was a brand new H2.'

'Pro'ly drunker 'an a skunk . . .'

'DAVID!' Susan is standing in the front door with the baby and the flashlight. He says goodnight to his neighbors and heads back to the house, going in through the garage door and locking it.

She is waiting for him at the interior garage door.

'I have candles over there if you'd grab them,' she says, pointing out a bench with drawers in the garage. 'I called the power company. They said about 45 minutes.'

David grabs the candles and puts his light back, walking back to the door by Susan's flashlight. She stands silently in the dark, waiting for him, and she turns and walks to the kitchen before he's back through the door.

Sitting at the kitchen table with the baby asleep in her arms, they speak in hushed voices by candlelight for what seems forever. Their two illuminated faces, Davey in silhouette, with the ethereal dancing of the flames are lost in time. Their words are soft, caring tones floating only to one another. There is no time, even, because it has stopped for them. In all of the infinite universe they are all that exist, suspended in static union with only breath in motion.

She speaks of her father and her childhood. She explains to him why she has been deceptive.

They are quiet and still when it happens. Ripped from a place of dual serenity, they wake as if from a dream when the electricity — the light — blares on again. The blackout lasted 90 minutes.

Susan looks at a hanging clock and says, 'That was a long 45 minutes.'

David only half smiles his concurrence.

<u>xxxvii</u>

Martin Grimes receives no response; only displeased glances. There's finally a lull in the others' conversation, and David takes advantage.

'I would like to know where the structure will be located,' he says.

A nearly relieved Jonathon Lafete answers 'Houston.'

'Texas?'

'Yes.'

Thinking Lafete was going to continue, David hesitates before asking, 'And what will be its main purpose?'

Jonathon Lafete smiles, looking at Elizabeth and Martin before focusing again on David. 'A jewelry store,' he says.

<u>xxxviii</u>

In the bedroom, David strips to his underwear, puts on pajama bottoms, and goes into the bathroom to brush his teeth. When he emerges Susan is pulling a nightgown over her head.

'Susan.'

She looks at him. Automatically adjusting her nightgown so it hangs free and isn't twisted. He stands shirtless with a look that stirs her, and she smiles in response to the tone of his deep voice, hoping that he wants her. She turns, her body first and then her head to look at him.

He stares back.

She steps to the bed and pulls back the covers. She looks into his eyes once again, taking the side of the nightgown into her fist, preparing to further entice him by hiking it up.

'I want a divorce.'

'But . . .' Susan's head shakes a little, but she doesn't realize it. That's all she says, looking confused.

'I know this seems odd; why I'm saying it now though. To do it later would be wrong. Because I've already decided. I have to leave you.'

'Why, David? Why?' The voice asking the question is the most painful he's ever heard.

'I'm not being fair to myself. I'm not being honest with you. Or Davey.'

'What?' She gets a grip on something within herself, and demands more because by yelling. 'Why? Why? WHY!?'

David delivers an explanation. He says, 'Because, Susan. I'm gay.'

<u>xxxix</u>

'You are not. That's absurd. Ridiculous.'

'I realize it's hard for you to hear the truth. I've denied it to myself for so long, but I am. I don't want you to be angry. I don't want you to think that this is somehow your fault. It just is what it is. It's who I am. I realized . . No. I accepted the fact today that for my sake, for all of our sakes, that I have to do what's right to be happy. So that years from now I'm not miserable, not bitter and full of regret, so I'm telling you. I would ...

'I already feel so relieved just having said it! I feel so good having admitted it to you. I would think that if you loved me, you'd accept it. You should be happy for me without putting yourself through any pain.'

'Be happy for you!? I think you're being childish and selfish and not making any sense! What about me? What about your son?'

'I'll always love you, Susan. And what's really going to change between us? Nothing that matters.

'And as to *my* son, how could I ever look him in the eye? Or tell him what to do? Or expect him to

68

respect me if he never knows me? How could I ever say, 'I love you no matter what,' if I don't trust him enough to give him the chance to love me the same way? And all because of some prideful deception.'

'That's fucking bullshit, David, and you know it. You spend a few hours alone with that bitch of a shrink and start spouting that you're ... that you're a fairy with no regard to your life or your family.'

'That's exactly what I'm thinking about, but you can't accept that because you're only thinking about yourself! You're the one being selfish! Do you have any idea how difficult it is for me to tell you this?'

'I'm sure you've been waiting for the perfect moment all fucking day, you asshole. Especially after...' She fights angry tears unsuccessfully. 'God damn it! You must think I'm a real fucking idiot! I wish I hadn't bled my heart out! I'd have saved my breath if I knew this was coming!'

'So you'd rather I be a lying hypocrite like you!? How many years did you lie to me about your father? . . .'

'How dare you . . .'

'. . . I knew there was something more to that story. After we got serious how many times did I ask about your father?' Speaking with a mocking falsetto, David says, '*Nothing to tell, I barely knew him, divorced my mom when I was young.*'

'. . . you fucking bastard, you . . .'

David's normal voice is accusative: 'It makes me wonder what else you've lied to me about through the years.'

'. . . shut up! Just stop your mouth before . . .'

'All you do is think about yourself! You *are* a

selfish liar!'

'Shut the fuck up!' Susan's hands are white knuckled fists at her side, standing by the bed. She launches herself at David as she demands his silence. Her arms lash out like wings, the right hammering the side of his jaw and the left pounding his chest.

He takes the blows without feeling them before catching her wrists, saying her name and asking her to stop. She struggles, writhing and enraged like a confined animal, uttering incoherent curses. David shoves her, hard, so that she falls on her back on the bed. She stops and stares at her husband, glaring at him with hurt and hatred.

David stands still, and sweat trickles down the center of his abdomen. He stares back at her.

He says, fighting his own emerging tears, 'This isn't what I wanted. Sorry about the timing. Sorry about everything. I'm sorry. But I am gay. And I want a divorce.'

He leaves the room without waiting for or wanting a response and slams the door. He goes downstairs to sleep, ignoring her cries from inside the bedroom.

<u>xl</u>

Susan calls his name as he turns to leave, but he doesn't pause. The door slams. All alone inside the bedroom she screams and cries.

He's dead to me now. This, she knows, she does not truly believe, but she likes to think it.

I'm going to destroy him. She plots and fumes, yet she cries herself to sleep.

CHAPTER EIGHT

THE LAST DAY (3)

<u>xli</u>

David Guy opens the closet door, thinking about all the turmoil that occurred after he came out. He has a hanger in his hand. He was going to pull it out to hang his coat but freezes, remembering.

Five days after his confession he moved out, sleeping those nights on the couch or the floor next to the crib. He's at the crib, saying goodbye to Davey, not knowing when or if he'll see him again. It will be months until the divorce. It will be months until the custody decision. Susan appears in the doorway.

'Haven't you left yet?'

He wants to respond with the same contempt and rhetoric: 'Does it look like it?' He simply says, 'No, I'm talking to our son.'

He receives a momentary glance from Susan then. It's the look that will define her in years to come.

It is a face fixed in rage with moist eyes threatening tears. There's a twitch, barely observable, at the left corner of her mouth. Those moist eyes are working, searching for some reason they can accept, but are forever stuck with confused and disbelieving stagnancy. Detached from the cause, these eyes are sad and possibly poignant, but they're definitely sad. They are pitiable, like a lost puppy in the rain.

The surface of the look glares, piercing David like a dagger. It causes him anger now, but in the future it will cause him pity.

After a long moment, having decided not to respond, she goes upstairs and waits for him to leave.

<u>xlii</u>

David stands before the closet with the door wide open. A coat is clutched in his left hand and a hanger in his right, and his eyes are cast to the floor. Beyond him hang a few coats and jackets, and more empty hangers dangle. On a shelf above the bar is a disorganized pile of gloves, mittens, scarves, and various types of hats. Sitting on the floor is a vacuum cleaner, a golf bag, and something else.

David's eyes focus on the mitten, finally recognizing it although he's been looking at it for minutes. He hangs his coat and bends to pick it up. Once it's in his hand he realizes it's not a mitten. It's a knitted driver cover; what he calls a golf club cozy.

David slides the hanging garments to the left, so they're not obscuring the city-like skyline tops of the clubs that jut from the golf bag. Knowing nothing of golf, he covers the largest club with the knitted cozy. He closes the closet door, turns, and walks to the phone. Hanging on the wall in the kitchen.

<u>xliii</u>

One ring. Two rings. Charles answers and says, 'Hello, Davey boy. Your son was just asking me to call you when the phone rang.'

'How're the roads?'

'Well, you know, I think they're fine, but we're not moving.'

'If everybody's going slow it's just because they're being careful.'

'No, no. We're literally not moving. Still. There must be an accident up ahead, but I can't see it.'

'I'll have hot cocoa ready when you get home. What do you want for dinner?'

'We stopped for take out at the Peking Duck, so thus Chinese.'

'I'll set the table.'

'Thanks, Davey boy. That's so kind of you.'

David can hear Davey in the background, who says, 'My name is Davey, too.' A smile comes to his face, and he hears, 'Let me talk to my Daddy.'

Charles says, 'Your son would like to speak with you.'

Laughing, David says, 'Well, put him on already, woman!'

He hears the phone being passed, and Charles says, 'Here you go, bud.'

<u>xliv</u>

'Hello, Daddy.'

'Hi, Davey. What's up?'

'Oh, I'm riding in the car. Daddy, Charles said if I don't have school tomorrow that we'll build a snowman.'

David looks over his shoulder and out of the dining room window to catch a glimpse of the falling snow, already expecting to see a snowman the next day. He asks, 'Did you get enough fortune cookies?'

Davey begins to giggle, and the dog barks twice. Davey shrieks, 'Sarah is licking me!'

'Davey,' David says, thinking the dog must be thirsty, 'Did you get enough fortune cookies?'

Davey, still giggling, says, 'Yes. I told the lady we needed four.'

'Good man, you remembered. I'll see you when you get home. I love you.'

'I love you, too, Daddy.'

David hangs up.

CHAPTER NINE

~FIVE YEARS EARLIER (2)

xlv

Three blocks from the T. Helmway building, living out of a few boxes, a giant suitcase, and a lackluster closet, David Guy has moved into a downtown apartment. It's been over three months since he last saw Davey, but he's beginning to consider his mediocre downtown flat as comfortable; not just bearable.

xlvi

Three months and a few days after the initial consultation with Pructor and Lafete concerning the Houston jewelry store, the first monthly project meeting is scheduled. Despite the walking distance, David always feels rushed living downtown, and this morning, although he is not, keeps thinking he will be late.

CHAPTER TEN

CHARLES

<u>xlvii</u>

David nearly stumbles into his office, too harried, and cumbersome with all that he's carrying. With a deep breath he's able to relax, slightly, after glancing at the digital clock on his desk. He has plenty of time. He doesn't have to be there for another ten minutes, and the meeting doesn't start for over an hour.

He sits down, his back hard against the chair, and stares at the blinking light on his phone. He has voicemail.

Breathing, relaxing, David sits for over two minutes thinking about listening to his messages, waiting for something before he does it. He is just, truly, relaxing. He reaches out with both hands. One grabs up the receiver, and the other, after the other's snatch, pushes the blinking button. Before he even hears automated instructions, David hears a knock at his office door, which is more than a quarter of the way open.

David drops the receiver back into place before identifying the person who has knocked, but he looks up instantly to see. He smiles, seeing the hand that's pushing the door open, and knowing before his brain is capable of telling him that he knows.

'Byron! How is it going this morning?'

'Ha, ha, man. You tell me.'

After a few moments of watching his friend, David's smile goes away before coming back bigger. Then he seriously says, 'I'm definitely ready.'

All of Byron's good humor seems to disappear. 'David, man,' he says, 'you better be.' His smile comes back, and he asks, 'Jonathon Lafete gonna be here?'

David looks at the work things he carried in, still out in various places on the top of his desk. He looks around, thinking.

'I don't know,' he says with a shrug of his shoulders. David begins to mentally organize, and then goes to moving things around to where they need to be, talking to Byron as he does so. 'I guess I'd expect him to be, but you never know.'

David dips into his portfolio, a rolled up satchel that actually holds more than it seems it should. The piles of paper are stacked like maps, but David deftly slides out the blueprints and sketches he needs for the meeting. He rolls the others up again, placing them on a nearby shelf.

'You should ride up with me,' David says. He sees the question in Byron's eyes and adds, 'Up to the meeting when I go. I have to get those condo specs for you, and they're up there. Better excuse than any, I'd say.'

Byron is nodding and backing out of David's office. 'Man, that sounds like a plan.' He slaps the frame of the door. 'Stop for me on your way up, man,' he says, heading down the hall.

David shouts, sliding pencils and other utensils

into a drawer, 'I will, I will. I need some coffee first, but don't you worry.

'Nope,' says David; now to himself and not shouting. 'Don't worry at all.'

xlviii

David stands outside the door to the conference room, talking to Byron Jenson. It's an inconspicuous way for Byron to check out the unknown faces attending the meeting. Much to Byron's disappointment, Jonathon Lafete does not attend.

David farewells Byron, bowing his head. He enters the conference room and closes the door.

xlix

Elmer Dean, before everyone is seated and in his swine-like manner, says, 'Everyone knows me and Marty,' indicating his fellow attorney, the other person present that's also named Martin.

'This is Elizabeth Cooper, Martin Grimes, and David Guy. This is Ralph Hapshat, Charles Grey, and Wendy Freeman.'

Elmer indicates who he means with combinations of different porcine gestures. He pulls out his chair and sits down.

After clearing his throat, Martin Grimes says, 'Well, I'd like to thank everyone for coming. Leading up to a project, typically, we'll meet like this once a month. After construction starts we'll meet weekly, or even daily, if necessary.'

After a nodding modicum of silence, the other Martin speaks. He says, 'Since construction is years away in time, this will be a rather preliminary meeting.' He surveys the faces of those sitting with him at the round table. Glancing at David before speaking again, he continues, 'I'm told that David has several design concepts to present to us.' His smile, for a moment, catches everyone's eyes. 'Is there anything anyone would like to contribute, before he begins?'

'We do, actually,' says Elmer Dean, 'and T. Helmway will be quite pleased. The lot has been acquired.'

'That is great news,' says Elizabeth, glancing at Martin Grimes.

Elmer says, 'Yes,' and begins distributing spiral bound notebooks. David grabs one of them up, lashing out for it like a whip. Elmer adds, 'The location is prominent in downtown Houston.'

Martin Grimes thumbs through his quickly before slapping it closed on the table. He asks, 'When will we receive financial information?' He looks from the two lawyers and glares for a moment at David, quickly, before looking back to them. David does not notice; Martin Grimes seems to be much more relaxed than he'd been at the initial consultation.

Elmer Dean, as though explaining the already explained, levels his gaze at Martin Grimes with a contented, patient expression, and answers, 'As soon as possible after the closing, Mr. Grimes.' After realizing that Martin Grimes will remain quiet, he prompts David to begin his presentation.

I

David finds it hard to control his enthusiasm, although he does; this meeting will eventually live in his memory as one of the best ever.

He has drawn several design concepts for the building, going simply on 'jewelry store' and 'Houston'. David looks up from his presentation materials and asks Elmer, 'I'd like to ask a few quick questions about the site first, if I may?'

A gracious Elmer Dean nods as he invites, 'Ask away, Mr. Guy.'

Ii

David has been flipping through spiral bound notebook pages, rapidly searching. He's been toggling between the first page and a map of downtown Houston.

David asks, 'This is *the* address?'

Elmer says, 'Yes,' with a patient smile, as though answering a rhetorical question.

David has a smile emerge, which he kills. He thumbs through his design sketches, deftly separating one from the stack.

David holds up the picture he's drawn; both lawyers smile. Martin Mackenzie says, 'It's right off the interstate; nearly at the corner of Dallas and Texas.'

liii

Martin Grimes frowns as he looks up and down a few times between a page in the notebook and David's sketch of the building.

Elizabeth Cooper notices the page he's on and turns to it in her own notebook. She smiles in amazement when looking up again at David's drawing.

Ralph Hapshat, Charles Grey, and Wendy Freeman (the three people whose name is all that David knows about them) for the most part all react the same way. Once they catch on, all three find the page of their spiraled pages. They then dumbly beam up at David and his drawing, but with the following exceptions:

Ralph Hapshat is first, beaming all the way. He's a dumb grin on his face before even looking down at the notebook.

Charles Grey's look is incredulous at first: a smart-ass look. He finds the page and looks back up, studying, and then the genuine smile.

Wendy Freeman is the last one to beam. Sitting apathetically, staring at David's drawing with a stern boredom on her face, she looks to Charles when he beams, and then notices the expressions of the others.

Charles leans in toward her and says, 'Turn to page five in your notebook, dear.'

'Huh,' she says, and then, 'Oh.' Seemingly embarrassed, and with furtive glances and a small apologetic smile to nearly every face she can see, Wendy Freeman flips to the page. She studies it with the same stern-bored look she had previously. Finally, after forever, and with those in the room having the air of having had to wait for her to catch up, she smiles at the large sketch David is holding for all of them to view. Though a dumb smile, it doesn't seem to ever reach her eyes. The nonexistent glistening of stern boredom never leaves them.

Still, in David's perception, she is dumbly beaming.

liii

David's presentation is brief. The plan to have a discussion over his various exterior sketches; for the group to decide which one would be best, was naturally, by course of fate, basically decided upon with the knowledge of the building's address. Once the sketch was put away, and once David's presentation was over, it was Elmer Dean who spoke.

'Perhaps everyone who hasn't been introduced already should introduce themselves,' he says. 'Ralph, you go first.'

Ralph, obviously a jovial man in David's estimation, glances at Elmer with serious questions. His gaze doesn't linger on David long, but a questioning look darts from Martin Grimes to Elizabeth Cooper. He chuckles, not unlike Santa Claus.

'No, I don't mind that, Mr. Dean,' says Ralph Hapshat, 'but I'd be a might appreciative if our hosts went first. Already think to know sharp and strappin' Mr. Guy here, but who're him and her?' Again he repeats a questioning look from Grimes to Cooper, before leveling the seriousness of his question on Elmer Dean.

Martin Grimes instantly coughs. Into a fist, he

82

does, and then introduces himself. He simply says his name, and David finds the attitude of his speech preoccupied.

Elizabeth Cooper has to introduce herself next, and a professional smile spreads across her lips. She effortlessly goes into her spiel.

'My name is Elizabeth Cooper,' she says. Her smile never falters. 'I'm the lead EAD on this project.' She notices Wendy Freeman's expression and feels the need to elucidate. 'Martin is also EAD. We're David's bosses. We're overseeing this project for T. Helmway.'

With the exception of her own, and of David's and the two attorneys', the other heads in the room nod as if they understand.

Ralph Hapshat says, 'Well, thank ye very much,' breaking the idiosyncratic bobbing of heads. His own seems to continue for another nod before he continues speaking.

liv

'Name is Ralph. Ralph Hapshat. Born 'n' raised 'bout 35 miles outside a Houston. Contractor by trade, so this board room shit . . .' He laughs. Looking at Elizabeth he says, 'Pardon m' French, ma'am.'

She smiles and nods, begging him to continue.

'This'll be m' third project with —'

Elmer Dean was furiously shaking his head, and the other Martin had jumped up from his seat.

'Well, damn near forgot. I ain't sposed t' say. These two guys from the law firm that pays the bills 're alright, though. Far 's I can tell.'

Martin Mackenzie sits back down, coughing.

Iv

'You have to remember to include space for the plumbing.' This is Wendy Freeman, who's there representing the company tasked with the plumbing. David ponders why electricians aren't at the meeting. He comes to discover that the logistics of breaking ground in a downtown concrete jungle, tapping into existing sewer systems, amongst other technical difficulties, is a financial and political project unto itself. He also comes to discover that the wiring is under Ralph Hapshat's purvue.

David's nodding as he says to her, 'I know how to draw architectural blueprints.'

Martin Grimes jumps in and asks the other Martin, 'So there aren't any specific specifications at all?'

Both lawyers shake their heads and answer simultaneously, 'No.'

'Mr. Grimes,' is added by Elmer Dean.

Martin Mackenzie repeats the directive that was spoken earlier: 'Mr. Guy and Mr. Grey are to work together. Essentially, the design is entirely their baby, if you would all pardon the phrase.'

'I've never had the opportunity to do interior schematics before,' says David. 'We normally just do exterior architecture. And I understand Mr. Grimes's question: all we have as direction is that it's a jewelry store?' At hearing his name spoken Martin Grimes scowls, but David misses it.

Both lawyers simply nod their reply.

Wendy Freeman says, as they are nodding, 'You have to include the plumbing in the schematics.' For some unknown reason, David thinks of a teenage girl chewing gum, blowing a bubble, and the bubble popping.

Charles Grey, patting her hand, leans over toward her and says, 'He knows that, dear.' Charles Grey is the sole proprietor of Grey Design. He's charged with the totality of the interior design of the building, and its exterior facade and accents.

The building is to be a unique construction; made-to-order inside and out, per the artists' loving hands.

CHAPTER ELEVEN

MARTIN GRIMES

lvi

Elizabeth walks past him into the hall to join the line. She takes up place as second handshake receiver, offering her friendly goodbye as well as a swift usher toward the elevators.

lvii

David finds himself the receiver of a short line of handshakes once the meeting breaks. Along with the handshakes are everyone's future-hopeful farewells.

lviii

Elmer Dean and Martin Mackenzie are on David simultaneously. They're formal but sincere. Elmer beams as he approaches Elizabeth, and, for a reason unknown to David, he thinks the expression a bit too much.

Ralph Hapshat genially taps him on the shoulder as he walks away. And, even though contact information was included in the spiral bound notebook each of them received, Charles Grey hands him a card. David watches him walk past Elizabeth Cooper and toward the elevators.

<h2 style="text-align:center">lix</h2>

'Excellent job, David, really.' This is Martin Grimes speaking. It seems odd to David that he's hung back inside the conference room, hovering near his chair. He isn't just giving a compliment, either; David feels there's more to come.

'Is there something wrong, Martin?' David asks.

'I hope not.'

David wonders if Martin Grimes could be any more ominous.

He picks up his things from the table, and, walking past David, he says, 'Come to my office for a minute.' He pauses outside of the door, in the hall near to Elizabeth Cooper. He looks back at David and says, 'Not now. Not if you're heading to lunch.'

David notices Elizabeth chatting with Ralph Hapshat and the lawyers from Pructor and Lafete. She eavesdrops on Martin Grimes, and, with a private glance to David, lets him know that something is up.

Elizabeth's glance slightly worries him. David is careful not to sound perplexed, however, as he says, 'I'm right behind you.'

lx

He's not ready for the hand that comes out of nowhere. He's not ready for the voice, either, that says, 'Again it's a pleasure.'

David takes the hand and shakes it, looking up into the beaming face of Charles Grey.

'I'm truly looking forward to working with you.'

David says, 'Oh,' as he's totally taken by surprise. When he saw the hand, he had to shift the things he's holding to his left hand. He's in front of the elevators, having just missed the ride up to the EAD floor with Martin Grimes. That's when he thinks :

He's not smiling. His eyes are beaming.

An elevator door opens with a ding, and David, nearly rude, jumps onto the elevator away from Charles. He recovers enough from his surprise to turn around and say, as the elevator doors begin to close, 'Likewise and also. I'll get in touch next week.'

lxi

Wendy Freeman, representing the plumbers, asks, 'Why aren't we getting on the elevator?'

Charles Grey replies, 'We want to go down, dear.'

lxii

'Close the door, please, David.' All of the typical pomp is absent from his voice.

88

David closes the door and instantly feels claustrophobic; bright shafts of light are coming through partway open slats covering the windows. There's also a continuous shadow around the edge of the room. They make the office seem darker than it actually is. He doesn't trust in speaking without revealing his anxiety, so he remains silent.

'I've never encountered this kind of situation before, David,' says Martin Grimes. 'I'm not quite sure how to handle it.'

There's a heavy and longer than a second second then.

'So I'm just going to play this message for you.' Martin Grimes puts his phone on speaker and dials into his voicemail.

The message begins, and it's a voice that David knows. It's Susan's voice.

lxiii

'This message is for Martin Grimes. This is Mrs. Susan Guy. I'm calling to let you know that my husband is a pervert. He doesn't like the taste of my pussy anymore. He sucks on the cock now.'

lxiv

He'd been feeling like he's being interrogated since closing the door. Sweating since then; trapped inside this shrinking office space. Even the shrill voice of Susan, and the meaning of her words, are only enough to slap him into attention.

Shame and embarrassment. An anger so much it has to be fury. David's first thought comes out as a statement :

'I'm not responsible for what Susan says and does. She's upset because of the divorce.'

lxv

His words hang like an ugly discomfort. He's aware he's stating the obvious, and he's aware that Martin is aware of the situation. David begins to question Martin's motives for playing the message.

lxvi

'I thought you should know. Hear it for yourself. I couldn't have *told* you what she said.'

'I can understand that.'

'Are you alright? Is there anything I can help you with?'

'No, thanks. I'm fine, though. Sorry, too. Her calling you is not appropriate.'

'What can you do, though, David? I have to think of T. Helmway's interests.'

'You don't have to worry. She'll calm down.'

lxvii

David detects that Martin Grimes is, slightly, uncomfortable. He hopes the feeling is due to the nature of the general situation.

Although he is, for certain, not entirely sure.

lxviii

'I'd appreciate it if you wouldn't tell anyone about this.'

'Of course I won't. The thought would never cross my mind, David.'

lxix

'Take my advice, David :
'Don't let this distract you.
'Now get back to work!'

lxx

He smiles. His attempt at levity, at least in David's opinion, fails.

CHAPTER TWELVE

ELIZABETH COOPER

lxxi

Alone on the elevator, riding back to his own floor, returning to his own office, David somehow keeps the demons out of his head; he keeps his head quiet.

Once back in his office, David maintains his peace. He does this by forging on, working ahead with the Houston jewelry store design. After awhile he puts this aside and works on other projects.

lxxii

It is later in the afternoon. Someone knocks as they step into his office.

David says, 'Hello, Elizabeth,' after looking up to see who it is. He pushes away from his desk, going to stand to greet her.

'Don't get up,' she says, shaking her head. She seems flattered, though, that he initiated the gesture. She praises his morning presentation with a flare poised only by herself; then she asks, approaching his desk, 'Are you working on it now?'

<u>lxxiii</u>

'What?' David's initially flustered. No member of the EAD team has ever just stopped by his office during the near decade of his employment, except for his own managing supervisor, and never unannounced. 'No. I'm working on the Lake Erie condos, but I have it ... right ... here.'

He clears away the work covering his desk, and grabs the structural blueprints for the jewelry store from a low shelf he can reach from his chair. They discuss his intentions for the edifice, and he finds himself glad for vetting his ideas through her.

'This is going to be something, David,' she says. She turns and walks away as though leaving, but closes the door and turns back to face him. No matter how she stands she is always posed and dignified, but when she speaks again her tone is seriously familiar. 'I was in Martin's office before the meeting this morning, and he played the message for me.'

David doesn't think his facial expression changes, but it must work somehow.

'No, David, you don't have to say anything to me,' says Elizabeth Cooper. 'It's unfortunate that he tends to be reactionary. I told him to forget it, so, for what it's worth, I wanted to let you know . . .'

David thinks there's more she wants to say, but he quickly thanks her.

She nods you're welcome and says, 'You can trust me, David.' Elizabeth Cooper turns and leaves.

<u>lxxiv</u>

David sits and thinks of what to make of the exchange, but he comes up blank. He looks at the time : 5:05. His head dully aches, his stomach growls, and instantly he decides that he's done working for the day. He gathers his things and heads for Byron's office.

CHAPTER THIRTEEN

BYRON

<u>lxxv</u>

'David! Come on in, man.'

Yearning for greasy food and a confidant, David doesn't delay asking the question: 'You wanna grab a beer before you head home?'

Byron's smile gets bigger. Toothier. 'Absolutely, man. Absolutely.'

<u>lxxvi</u>

Low hanging glass shaded lamps float above the tables, booths and stools in the bar. Its smoky air is inviting and pleasant. The mid-scale suburban tavern they liked was equidistant from both of their neighborhoods. It was equidistant, before David moved into the city.

David doesn't mind travelling so far. He wants to retreat from the constancy of action and noise downtown, because, he thinks, *sometimes you want to go.*

lxxvii

It's been nearly eight years since Byron had been hired on by T. Helmway. He and his wife, Miriam, had moved up from Atlanta after he'd been taken on.

It's been nearly eight years since David struck up a conversation with Byron after he appeared at the water cooler during 11 a.m. coffee break. That led to double dates, dinner parties, and the like.

Wife came to work with wife, because of, early on at one of these occasions, something that Mrs. Susan Guy says.

lxxviii

Miriam Jenson says, in a way, because the specific words she uses are not known, something to indicate that she's looking for work. Lackadaisically.

'Where I work always seems to be hiring,' responds Susan.

lxxix

'Man, that's really fuckin' wicked.' Byron Jenson picks up the heavy handled mug and takes a gulp of his beer.

David asks, 'On whose part, hers or his?' He's just told Byron about the voicemail she'd left for Martin Grimes.

The mug is still at Byron's mouth. He brings it down and, through foam, says, 'Man. Both of them, man.'

David tells him about his visit from Elizabeth Cooper.

lxxx

'For some reason I love that woman,' he says.

The bartender drops off extra crunchy hot wings and a side of onion wings.

'Thanks, Keith.' David eats a few onion rings before indicating to Byron that he can help himself. Byron thankfully shakes no. David swigs from his beer. He says, 'He's probably told everyone.'

'Man. Listen, man. You can't worry about that bullshit. Especially when it comes from him.'

lxxxi

Byron downs the rest of his beer.

'I need to wash down the rest of these onion rings.' David does the same and asks, 'You want one?'

'Please.'

lxxxii

He returns with the beers. They sip in silence for what seems minutes.

'What's Susan been saying at work?'

'Man. You really wanna know?'

'I asked. Didn't I?'

Byron takes a drink. 'She got an official reprimand yesterday.'

'Maybe that pushed her to call Grimes.'

'Don't, David, man. Don't.' Byron looks up into David's eyes. He says, 'Don't waste your time finding excuses for Susan, man.'

lxxxiii

Byron takes a drink. 'Miriam's always sayin' you deserve better.'

'I deserve to be happy.'

'Don't we all, man? Don't we all?'

lxxxiv

Byron lifts his glass and finishes his beer. David does the same.

He says, 'I'm going to have one more.' He asks, 'You?'

Byron says, 'Nah. Three's a perfect number. I have to get home to Miriam and the baby.'

'Thanks for having a drink with me.'

'Anytime, man. Anytime.' He stands and throws money onto the table. 'Until tomorrow.'

CHAPTER FOURTEEN

TWO DAYS LATER

<u>lxxxv</u>

I am Susan. I am Woman. I am Mother.

<u>lxxxvi</u>

'Who the hell are you?' asks Susan.

'You should not be doing that.'

'I'm not hurting anyone here. Just mind your own business.'

'I'm calling 911.'

'You fucking asshole.' Susan stands up and says, 'Do not call 911.'

The man dials 911 and says, 'You're going to wait here until the police arrive.'

'The fuck I am.' Susan drops the can of spray paint and begins to walk away.

<u>lxxxvii</u>

The man on the phone gets in her way, and with

his free hand he clamps down on her arm just below her left armpit. Susan goes to slap at him with her right, and he moves his head out of the way as he shouts the address for the T. Helmway building into the phone. She struggles to get free from his grip. Mustering gumption, like pulling a toy car backwards so it'll roll on its own across the floor, Susan hears a voice behind her as she goes to surge.

'Joe?'

Susan would have broken free, but a pair of dark arms restrain her around her torso. She kicks and writhes in a short violent burst, but the three arms hold her. She gets a hold on the arms about her, and Joe lets go of her arm.

When she touches the arms holding her she recognizes them. She knows who it is, and her will to struggle somewhat abates. People she knows know, so she figures herself caught. She turns, and the arms let her turn within them, until she's looking up into the face of Byron Jenson.

lxxxviii

Byron lets go of her. He doesn't want to believe that he's come upon this scene. He glances at the side of David's car, at the can of spray paint on the ground, and back at Susan's face. There's still a fight in her.

'How do you want to do this, Susan?' The question seems enough to keep her still. He feels the weight of his cell phone and grabs it to call David.

<u>lxxxix</u>

He's working through his lunch today, although he does have a plan to lunch on fruit, a sandwich and leftovers. These plans change, however, when — two bites into his pear — the work phone rings. Only twice, but he's already done having set the pear down and wiping juice from his hands. He's about to pick up the pear and start eating it again when his cell phone rings. The incoming call is from Byron Jenson.

'Byron! What's up? Did you just call my office phone?'

Rarely sounding so serious, 'You need to come out to your car, man,' says Byron.

<u>XC</u>

I am Susan. I am Woman. I am Mother.
It is so just paint. No big deal.
Tattle-tell tattle-tale, hanging on a bull's tail; when the bull takes a P, you get a cup of T ... *He's choosing him over me.*

<u>xci</u>

'Yeah, that's it,' she says. 'Call him, big man Byron. Call him! Call the no good son of a bitch! Tell him to get his ass out here! This is fucking great. Just call him. Yeah!'

<u>xcii</u>

David thinks he hears a voice he'll never forget. He asks, 'Is that Susan?'

Byron answers, 'Man. Just get down here, David.'

<u>xciii</u>

It's a pleasant, late spring day in June. The kind of day that he prefers to stay inside during lunch, because the temptation to then not go back in is that much.

David rushes out of the T. Helmway building and into the parking lot. His senses are greeted by gentle breezes, sounds of traffic, the song of robins, an earthy odor of awakening and newness that's gone by summer, and the overpowering smell of freshly mown grass.

How can anything be wrong on a day like this?

But, off in the distance, there is.

People he knows are standing next to his car, although he can't see it. He just sees their heads, floating and milling above the sun-glinted roofs of vehicles. He stops, observing, watching the heads nearly circling, like they're above the hedges of some automotive labyrinth.

There's a police cruiser coming. He can see the flashing lights as it pulls into the parking lot.

No more than two minutes, and he begins to head to his car again.

Chapter Fifteen

HUNTER & STARK

<u>xciv</u>

David sees the heads of two police officers rise into view with the lights at the top of their vehicle. They survey the scene before wading in amongst the cars towards the heads of Byron, Susan, and a coworker. He doesn't know his name, but David recognizes him as he moves to meet the approaching police officers. Byron seems to circle about Susan, as though he thinks she might bolt, and they get arranged so that her back is to him when he's nearly halfway there.

The space to the passenger side of David's car is vacant, and as he steps into it he kicks a can of spray paint that's on the ground. The coworker that he recognizes, but whose name he doesn't know, is talking to one of the police officers, loudly enough so that no one hears the sound of the rolling can. The other police officer has noticed him, but Byron is still staring Susan down, when David looks at his car.

Painted against the metallic mint green paint canvas of his Volkswagen Golf, in pink, are the letters *Q U E F*. Because it's almost funny to David, mostly funny, he begins to laugh.

XCV

I guess she used a good color.

XCVI

David's laughter fades quickly away, because Susan hears him. She slowly turns to look at him. David feels Byron's eyes on him, and he turns his head away from Susan's face to look into those eyes.

Susan's mouth works. A voice that isn't hers says, 'Wouldn't you know it. The nigger and the faggot.' She spits on the ground.

XCVII

She hears the words like everyone else within range does : like they're spoken by someone else. They're constructed somewhere in her brain and sent directly out of her mouth. Instantly she thinks: *Insert foot*; she supposes if circumstances were different, that if she hadn't just been caught spray painting *QUEER* on her husband's car, that she'd apologize.

As it is, she goes into a rage.

XCVIII

Susan screams, 'You fucking cocksucker!' at David.

The second police officer reveals her sex, moving toward Susan and shouting, 'You need to calm down, ma'am.'

Susan screams, 'I'm going to fucking kill you!'

Her partner breaks away from Joe to back her up as she forces Susan up against the car and places her in handcuffs. After briefly consulting with each other, the male police officer puts Susan into the back of their cruiser.

<u>xcix</u>

David answers, 'Yes, I want to press charges,' when asked. The officers' names are Trish Hunter and Lee Stark. It's Officer Hunter that officially queries him, while Officer Stark stands next to the cruiser, the back window down, his police pad flipped open, questioning Susan.

When their official business is over, again Hunter and Stark briefly consult. He walks up to David.

'Your wife would like to speak with you, sir.'

<u>c</u>

She's been crying. She says, 'You have to pick Davey up from daycare at five.'

He says, 'I'll have to stay at the house tonight.'

'It's your house, too,' she says. 'David,' she says, searching his face and debating with herself, 'will you bail me out?'

David viciously says, 'No,' and immediately feels

sorry for it. Apologetically, he says, 'I can't, Susan.'

She starts to cry again. She says, 'You're not the man I married.'

With his head shaking in anger, with a bitterness uncharacteristic of himself, and remembering what already seems a forever ago thing she'd asked him, David mocks her, asking, '*Why, David? Why?*' And then, quickly, he answers, 'No, I am. You're not the woman I married.'

She spits at him.

CHAPTER SIXTEEN

THE NEXT WEEK

<u>ci</u>

Sitting in his car outside the building, David glances down at the business card. Besides the obvious address and phone number, it simply says Grey Design, with the words *Interiors and Landscapes* below.

The wind is rustling lore out of the trees as David closes the door and locks his car, for which he'd wasted no time in getting the graffiti painted over. This part of the city, the university and businesses at the edge of campus, always strikes as ultra picturesque, evoking a powerful notion of loss for something never had, and a longing to again be where never been. Like walking into a pretty postcard, it's being instantly transported to a dream place of unwavering beauty and tranquility. At least until a passing vehicle blares its horn at a crossing student.

Chic and modern, but at the same time unpretentious and inviting, the steel and glass storefront of Grey Design, with its old fashioned rectangular awning shortly extending over the sidewalk, is noticeable yet blends with the other red-bricked buildings along the street. Inside it's minimalistic; mostly clean open space. Artistic furniture : two chairs and a small sofa, interesting and comfortable looking, is arranged in a corner around a small table. On the table are the current issues of *Contract* and *Lawn & Landscape*. The walls are hung with photographs of interior spaces and external landscapes; David supposes they're examples of the business's work.

Upon entering a twenty-something young lady wearing glasses and standing behind a high and long narrow glass counter-table looks up smiling and says, 'Good afternoon. May I help you?' Only a laptop is on the table-counter in front of her.

'David Guy. I'm here to meet with Mr. Grey.'

She walks around the rectangular glass-top and extends her hand. She says, 'I'm Mr. Grey's personal assistant. Lily Tafta.'

With a slight lift of the binder and large portfolio containing blueprints in his hands, David emphasizes his inability to shake hers.

'I figured it was you but didn't want to presume,' she says. 'Please, have a seat, and I'll let Charles know that you've arrived.'

'I must be obvious,' says David, walking to one of the two chairs in the corner. Then, in response to Lily, he says, 'Of course; thank you.'

She disappears through a door. David hadn't noticed it because she'd been standing in front of it, but now he can see it. From where he sits it's hard to make out the glass-top of the counter-table; so it seems the laptop is floating in front of the door.

<u>cii</u>

Charles emerges from behind the door with Lily following. She returns to her laptop.

'David, welcome,' says Charles. 'Did you have any trouble finding the place?'

'No, not at all.'

'That's good. Many of my clients are of an older persuasion, and they seem to have troubles more often than not. I think it has something to do with being around so many young people, but I can't be certain. Personally, I find it invigorating.'

David can't help but smile. He says, 'OSU is my alma mater, and I used to know the entire campus like the back of my hand. I don't ever make it over this way that much anymore, but you know what they say : it's like riding a bike.'

It's Charles's turn to smile. 'Oh, I'm sure,' he says. 'Whenever you're ready, if you would be so kind as to follow me.'

David stands and grabs his things leaning against the side of the chair. 'I am ready, sir.'

Charles laughs. '*Sir?* Did you hear that Lily?'

Without looking up from the laptop she says, 'Yes I did, Charles.'

Holding the door behind Lily open for David, Charles says, 'That word reminds me of my father; boy did I ever despise that old coot. Please, I must insist you call me Charles.'

<u>ciii</u>

Expecting the door to open onto a hall, David steps into another large open space. There are no support columns and no walls, except the four exteriors.

So this is where all the real work is done, he thinks to himself. David asks, 'So if this is your showroom and workspace, what do you call that entrance area out there?'

'Reception,' answers Charles.

<u>civ</u>

Warehouse-like, Grey Design's workspace is easily three times the area of reception. David thinks it resembles an expo or convention by its design and arrangement. There's a spot or a table for possibly every task that could ever need doing, with appropriate resource materials near at hand : a paint swatch station, various fabric samples, tile samples, wallpaper and other finishes. By the floor-to-ceiling windows there's an organized collection of topiary samples. There's also a loft; metal stairs, made of a steel alloy, purposefully weathered and ancient looking, rises along the wall opposite the windows. They lead to a balcony that spans the width of the room from wall to window, and it's constructed from the same steel as the stairs. A single thick cylinder of the steel stretches about four feet above the edge as a handrail. The handrail seems to float like a perpendicular trestle for three doors, which open off the loft behind it. It's so much, so thoroughly over the top yet simple and perfect, that he doesn't quite believe it.

David is standing still, frozen, surveying this never before seen environment, and his attention becomes focused on the doors. Charles notices and steps up to his side.

Pointing, first at the left most door, Charles says, 'Supply room, private office, and the one nearest the stairs houses the facilities.'

Understanding with a nod, David asks, 'Those plants ... they seem impractical. Not just to keep them alive; how do you keep up with all the pruning?'

'It's a hobby. My first love, really. They're impressive for show, and I find the work a total stress reliever.'

'They're definitely impressive.'

'Thank you, David. Please,' he says, indicating that David should follow, 'we'll work over here.' He leads David to a bare table, and David unrolls the blueprints in his portfolio. Charles says, 'I've only seen pictures, but that mall is nothing to what this is going to be.'

'The Buckeye Mall in Akron?'

'Yes, David.'

David nods and says, 'Thanks.' He asks, 'Did you do some work in Akron that impressed Jonathon Lafete?'

'Akron? No, I've never done any official work in Akron.'

'Oh.' David wants to push for the sake of curiosity, but he doesn't.

Charles waits a tick, though, and says, 'My father's parents are from Akron. I'm from California, but always spent the summers with my grandparents here in Ohio. Jonathon's parents lived across the street from them.'

David's head cocks up, and he meets Charles's eyes.

Charles says, 'They've moved. Obviously.'

A question comes into David's eyes. It's because of the way Charles had said obviously : as though David should know they've moved. Charles sees the question; so realizing that David doesn't know his expression changes.

David looks away. He asks, 'You're from where in California?'

'Oh,' says Charles. 'We had a house just outside of Los Angeles County.'

'Interesting.' David asks, 'So you know Lafete personally?'

They lock eyes again.

Charles smiles and says, 'Yes.' He looks for a moment longer into David's eyes. He says, 'Actually, I don't mind telling you. My father died when I was a freshman in high school, and that summer we moved in with my grandparents. Jonathon and I were rather inseparable throughout high school.' He looks up at the air. He says, 'Ah, you know. The good ole days.'

David asks, 'Is he still one of your close friends?'

'Of course!' shouts Charles. 'How do you think I got this job?'

He smiles. He can't get over how Charles's eyes always seem to beam. To twinkle. David says, 'Obviously from your marvelous talent. Look at this studio! Martha Stewart would be extremely proud of you.'

'Please,' Charles says, 'I put that woman to shame.'

'I don't know. She is Martha Stewart.'

They laugh together.

<u>CV</u>

'Promise me something, David?'

Still laughing: 'Sure.' Not laughing, he asks, 'What?'

'If you ever hear anything about me, know that it is not true.'

CHAPTER SEVENTEEN

THE LONG PAST ROUTINE YEARS

<u>cvi</u>

David constantly hops through the next six months. He keeps up with his other work projects, but he's always collaborating with Charles on the jewelry store. The divorce hearings begin, and they're closely followed by the custody trial.

Expecting full custody, David is shocked by the judge's decision. 'With an aware and deliberate reckoning,' he'd said, awarding Susan weekend visitation rights.

Somewhat disappointed, but the first to acknowledge that a boy needs his mother, David finds ways to entertain himself on the weekends. Natural as their rapport, his Friday and Saturday evenings evolve to be spent with Charles. Not working.

A fact he keeps quite discreet, especially from his ex-wife.

<u>cvii</u>

'A lot of people say to renovate the interior first,

but I think if I do the exterior first it'll motivate me enough to realize, although it takes time, that I'll eventually get the inside changed to the way I want it.'

In front of Charles's house are scaffolds, and his lawn is littered with carpentry things the first time that David sees it.

'I searched for three years for this house.'

'Really?'

Charles is nodding, petting Sarah. 'I can't wait until it's finished.'

cviii

On the first time David's inside of it, the first floor walls are all still up.

'It took so long because I wanted one that still had most of the original crown molding. This one had all of the original woodwork, and but one room had the original wallpaper. Very worn in certain places but overall well-taken care of. I lucked out when I found her.'

cix

'And this is the dining room,' announces Charles.

They've walked into the dining room through the door that enters from the living room. The only other door leads to the kitchen, because the door to the veranda is currently, and since being originally built, out of the kitchen. The French doors are constructed and the kitchen door sealed up during interior renovations, when the walls are removed. His first time inside, due to the walls, although the large window does alleviate the illusion to a small degree, the table seems to take up the entirety of the room. The scale of table to room, especially this first time he sees it, and then forever after as a fond memory, makes him think of the date scene in Batman. Keaton and Basinger sitting at opposite ends of that ridiculously long table, so that it takes Mr. Wayne nearly a full minute to walk the salt down to Vicki Vale.

Too bad it wasn't in the script to have her ask for the pepper after he sat back down again. Oh merry melodies.

CHAPTER EIGHTEEN

THE LONG PAST ROUTINE YEARS (2)

<u>CX</u>

'I don't know if you can do better than the first time, Charlie boy. That shrimp was something else. What are we having?'

Charles just smiles.

<u>cxi</u>

It's the third dinner that David is having with Charles in his home. As previously, the dog, Sarah, sleeps like a white and brown bear directly in front of the door to the living room. Charles revels in the pomp and circumstance of his hospitality; he's humble and gracious, but shows off at the same time.

As previously, they move after eating to the veranda to enjoy the summer night breeze, the quiet sound of crickets, Sarah's light snoring — she wakes almost preternaturally to move from room to room when Charles does, only to fall asleep again — and the rhythmic clink of chain tapping chain as they rock.

They sit next to each other on a hanging wooden

swing with the sleeping dog at their feet and full glasses of brandy in hand. David is on his second glass when Charles asks about his sister. All he knows is that she died young.

David looks over at Charles. He's unconsciously twirling his brandy glass while fondly watching Sarah.

CXII

David says, 'I want to tell you more about my sister.'

Charles looks into his eyes. Sober, there and still, he says, 'If you feel you need to.'

'I do, Charles.'

And so he begins the story.

He says, 'She caught me with the boy who lived across the street. That's how it all started.'

CXIII

Linda. Always struggling to not be shaded by her brother's shadow. Who followed him everywhere. Then by their teens he was her idol. Her main role model. She had a drinking problem. David knew and kept it secret from their parents.

CXIV

'I think about it now and think they must have

known. How couldn't they? Everything else they seemed to know as if by magic! To this day I don't get it.'

'Wait a few years. The easiest facts for anyone to deny are the ones that parents don't want to accept about their children. If you ask me it's a shame.'

CXV

High school came. So did the boy across the street.

'He was my age. I was a boy then so I think of him as a boy.'

CXVI

Playing doctor. Really.

'There was a stethoscope involved. We had biology together.'

CXVII

'Spare me all the gory details, David.'

'Obviously — I already said she caught us — Lin wasn't spared them.'

CXVIII

Then the monster she turned into.

CXIX

'It became my fault she drank, that's what she would say. But I had that over her head — her drinking — and she had this over mine. I was mortified by the thought of my parents knowing. I mean, Lin's reaction alone . . . it made me feel so . . . well, alone.'

'I know what you're talking about.'

Then her accident.

'It was ugly what she said to me. I try to tell myself she didn't mean it, but she did. Then she died. Of course I blamed myself. And I had no one to talk to about it. I wouldn't even look at the boy across the street anymore. And I buried it so deep so I wouldn't have to remember.'

CXX

That didn't work, though. The words to describe it struggle past his lips.

'Everything reminded me of it. Everything. I fought it and thought I had won. But I hadn't. I was just a shell.'

CXXI

Not empty. Full of regret the way a shell on the beach is full of the sound of that which created it.

And when he finishes, in tears, he looks at Charles. He doesn't know what, but he needs something.

<u>cxxii</u>

'The past is never fully relegated, David. It can't be. Nor should it be.'

'Why not?' To himself, through his tears, he sounds like a child.

'Because life's too short.'

'I dream about Lin, Charles.' David pauses; collects himself. 'When I dream about her I'm at the scene of the accident. In reality I only saw pictures of the mangled car, but I'm there anyway watching it happen. Screaming in silence. And she's there. All bloody. And I take her hand. It's warm and sticky and very weak. And I look at her. She looks at me. And she smiles. And she looks like a little girl again. Then her weak hand goes totally limp. And I know she's dead. But her eyes are still open. Staring at me like she knows something that I don't.'

<u>cxxiii</u>

This is David's confession. Another triangle. Linda to David to Charles. Instantly part of the good ole days.

Charles sets down his brandy glass to enshroud David with his embrace. He rocks him as they rock on the wooden porch swing, the dog oblivious, absorbing his sobs.

Chapter Nineteen

THE LONG PAST ROUTINE YEARS (3)

<u>cxxiv</u>

It's a prehistoric summer. Back when a summer is a day and a day is a summer.

The waves are roaring onto the beach. It's a soothing yet furious sound that's always heard in the background, even if you have to listen to hear it. The sun is so bright outside it seems a blinding light. They're playing on the sun porch. It's the brightest room in the house, but with the opaque shades down nothing compared to the eye-watering squint of the outside, reflecting up from white sand like a mirror.

There's a hard cardboard oven and a hard cardboard refrigerator. There's a baby table with stuffed animals in the baby chairs around it. It's set for tea with tiny cups and saucers made of plastic. There's a plastic stick of butter. He opens the refrigerator. She's put a miniature plastic can of green beans in the cardboard fridge.

'Sissy,' he says, 'these don't go here!'

'That's where I want them.'

'But they don't go there.'

As she takes the miniature plastic can of green

beans from him she says, 'They're mine!'

beans from him she says, 'They're mine!'

CHAPTER TWENTY

THE LONG PAST ROUTINE YEARS (4)

<u>CXXV</u>

Time, as whatever units of time encompassed within it — units that are infinitely definable — flees to the past. Time flees to memory, too.

But only if it is known.

Or knowable.

CHAPTER TWENTY ONE

THE LONG PAST ROUTINE YEARS (5)

<u>CXXVI</u>

The renovations to Charles's house are complete. David and Davey, now five years old, have moved in with him.

<u>CXXVII</u>

Approximately three months have passed since the move. Every one of those weekends, meaning each of those Fridays and Sundays, David has been the one there with Davey when Susan picks him up and drops him off.

<u>CXXVIII</u>

Charles says, 'She better not say one wrong word, because I will not hold back on telling her exactly what I think.'

'Whatever happened to *Kiss me an—*'

'Don't sing, David. I'm being serious.'

'Yes. Well. And you're worrying too much.'

'Whatever. We're still adjusting — along with Davey — to living together. And I think this is too soon.'

'Oh, Charlie boy! Please. I think you're really a little envious.'

'What are you talking about?'

'You're not even a little upset that you didn't get asked to go to this thing?'

'What?'

David catches Charles's eye with a look that tells him to come on, get real, and think about it.

Charles does think, and he becomes honest. 'Maybe a little! But why do I have to deal with your psycho ex-wife?'

'She's not psycho!' David takes a deep, calming breath. 'You can handle her if she runs her mouth, so don't worry about it. I have to get to the airport.'

They kiss.

David says, 'I love you.'

'Love you, too. Have a safe trip.'

<u>CXXIX</u>

There are mystery men present in Texas. David is not introduced to them. They're wearing hand-sewn tailored suits and saying things like 'innovative design' and 'beyond expectations.'

Charcoal grey pinstripe, fat as a bird, whose red tie and breast-pocket kerchief match, says, 'David Guy, let me shake your hand, son. You accomplished the goal we had in mind for this building. I'm personally congratulating you on an outstanding job.'

David says, 'Thank you very much, sir. I did my best.'

The fat bird — the raptor — though the same height as David, looks down upon him as he speaks.

'Who are you?' asks David.

The fat cock stuffed into charcoal grey pinstripe feathers smiles, chuckles under his breath, and with a dismissive shake of his avian head — his beady evil eyes always looking for prey — turns and walks away.

David looks over at the people he knows: Theodore Helmway, Elizabeth Cooper, Jonathan Lafete, and Ralph Hapshat. Only Lafete gazes in return, with eyes that say to not ask questions.

His mobile rings. It's Charlie Boy; given the time it means that back home Susan has picked up Davey for the weekend. The thought brings a smile to David's perplexed face. David answers, 'How did it go, Charles?'

'Never again, David. I have too much to worry about without having to put up with that cunt's abuse. There's no doubt that woman is fucking nuts, not stable, ignorant, and devoid of any compassion! If Davey was my son she'd never get him on the weekend, no matter what the court says.'

David asks, 'What'd she say?'

'I don't want to think about it right now. I'll tell you when you get home on Sunday. I'm so glad you'll be back when she drops him off. Anyway, how's it going down there?'

'Extremely well. We're about to head to dinner, I think.'

'Call me later, David.'

'I will.'

<u>CXXX</u>

Charles will tell David: 'Now I smiled and waved at her after I walked outside. She had the window up and never got out of the car.'

'I told you she wouldn't get out of the car. She never does.'

'And you know your son insists on struggling with that suitcase—'

'He does not struggle, Charles. He's expressing his determination. You're just impatient.'

'He must be determined, or as stubborn as his father. I think that thing was a quarter of his weight. Anyway, so I hung back, watching him struggle, and I wasn't paying much attention to Sarah.'

<u>CXXXI</u>

The dog.
'I love Sarah, Mommy.'
Look at that monster.
'I love Sarah, Mommy.'
He never said it was a Saint Bernard.
'I love Sarah, Mommy.'
I know what movie we'll be watching this weekend.

<u>CXXXII</u>

'I didn't realize she rolled down her window until she shouted, *Don't let that fleabag mutt piss on my car.*'

'What did you say?'

'Well, I said, in my friendliest voice, *Don't worry, Susan, dear, she is a she, and she is a pure breed.* Then she said, *You're not an old lady, asshole. Don't call me dear.* Now this is where it gets good. Davey shouted, *Mom, don't call Charlie applesauce*!'

'What?' David asks, laughing, 'where'd he get that from?'

'I have no idea, but it was priceless. And it pissed her off. She literally screamed, *Just get him in the fucking car*! Davey went, *Mommy*! We were at the car by then, and I opened the door, and Davey was trying to tell me how to buckle him into that confusing booster seat she has. So I ignored her until I got him all buckled in. Then I smiled and put out my hand and said — again in my very friendliest voice — *Hi, Susan. I'm Charles.* Are you ready for this?'

'Yes, Charles! Just stop with the suspense and tell the story!'

'She said, *I'm not going to touch you. I don't even like you touching my son.* Then she mumbled something.'

'Oh, now I can't wait. I know that got under your crawl.'

'I said, *I'm sorry, what did you say? I couldn't make it out.* She said, *I just called you a pervert.*'

'Enough with the dramatic pause! What did you say?'

'I said — still as reasonable Charles — *Do you really think you should speak that way in front of your son?*'

'I can't stand it when people refer to themselves in the third person.'

'Whatever, I'm telling a story. I get to use some poetic license.'

'Okay, okay! What did Susan say?'

'She went off, let me tell you!'

'For the love of God! What did she say?'

'She said, *Who the hell are you to tell me how to behave in front of my son? When that miracle happens and you and my husband have your own child then maybe I'll accept some advice. Until then, I'd just as soon not exchange words with you.*'

'Oh, what a bitch.'

'I wouldn't be so proud of your psycho bitch ex-wife. She's lucky I kept my cool. I looked her right in the eye, and I said, *He's not your husband anymore, dear. He's mine now.*'

'I knew you'd have to antagonize her.'

'What did you expect? She should've kept a civil tongue in her mouth.'

'What did she say after that?'

'Well if looks could kill I'd be dead, I know that much. She, like, growled, *shut the fucking door*! I told Davey bye, then I smiled at her and gave her a gay little wave. *See you Sunday, dear*, I said. Then I shut the door. She left, flipping me the bird as she drove away.'

'Did she really?'

'No, but I wish she had. She would have done something like that if it was a movie or something. Really, David, you should be more concerned about her behavior. At the very least I would document every nasty thing she says in front of Davey, and I'd let Simon know as well as that family court welfare chick. I mean, who knows what kind of psychological damage she's causing him.'

Chapter Twenty Two

THE LONG PAST ROUTINE YEARS (6)

<u>cxxxiii</u>

The unusual events of that week begin on Tuesday morning.

<u>cxxxiv</u>

It's the week after David's trip to Texas for the Houston jewelry store's groundbreaking that the rumors begin. It's a week after that when it's a fact. Joyce Smitley — EAD member and Byron Jenson's managing supervisor — is retiring.

<u>cxxxv</u>

David arrives at the usual time that Tuesday. He hasn't set the things he's carrying down when he notices someone has put a newspaper on his desk. He halts in putting down the things he's carrying when he sees a rather large headshot of Charles beaming at him in black and white from the front page. He glances at the headline, nearly just dropping the things he's carrying, and snatches up the newspaper as quickly as a striking serpent. He looks at the date, and it's today's paper. He reads the headline again: LOCAL MAN SUSPECTED OF AKRON TEEN'S MURDER NOW POSSIBLY PA SERIAL KILLER

'Good morning, David.'

Hearing a voice startles him, and he jumps. He tries to hide the newspaper behind his back as he turns to face Martin Grimes, who's standing in the doorway to his office.

'Martin.' David seems out of breath, and it takes him an extra second to put the appropriate smile on his face. 'Good morning.'

Martin has never looked so thrilled — or awake — this early in the morning. He says, 'Well, just wanted to say good morning.' He raps a couple times on the doorframe of David's office door and walks on — down the hall — bellowing a perfectly friendly sounding, 'Have a great day!'

CXXXVi

Per the typical T. Helmway fashion, Joyce Smitley's replacement is assigned at least a month before her final day of work. She helps to train — and she helps to choose — her replacement. Following so closely after the start of the Houston jewelry store's construction phase, there is little doubt in anyone's mind that David Guy will get the promotion.

And he does.

CXXXVII

From the Columbus *AM CONCERNED GAZETTE,* June 20th, 2000 (page 1):

**LOCAL MAN SUSPECTED OF AKRON TEEN'S
MURDER NOW POSSIBLY PA SERIAL KILLER**

M. Paris Gein-Brewt, staff writer – Reports obtained from the Commonwealth of Pennsylvania State Police confirm that Charles Grey, 40, is a 'person of interest' in their investigation of a mass murderer known only by the moniker The Puritan. In coordination with the FBI and Ohio's own State Police, forensic investigators have confirmed that DNA evidence identifies The Puritan as the slayer of Corey Lafete, 16, from Akron. He was last seen in 1982 with his brother, Jonathon Lafete, a partner with the law firm Pructor and Lafete, and Charles Grey. Mr. Grey owns and operates Grey Design Interiors and Landscapes in the University district. He resides in Woodland Park.

CXXXVIII

David reads the article twice. He reads it again before calling Charles.

Charles answers, 'Yes, David, I've heard.'

'What?' David is confused because the *AM CONCERNED GAZETTE* is a newspaper they rarely read. 'How? Have you read it?'

'No, but I had it read to me.'

'How?'

'Jonathon called me. Whoever this Gein-Brewt woman is — well — I don't know. I'm very angry, but Jonathon said the best thing, I think.'

'What's that? What did he say?'

'It won't really hurt my business; anyone who can

133

afford me should be smart enough to not believe a lie.'

David is silent for a moment. He finally says, 'But still, Charles. Your reputation.'

'I know, Davey boy, I know. But how does the saying go in Hollywood?'

David laughs a short laugh. He asks, 'Which one?'

'There is no such thing as bad publicity.'

'Yeah. I guess that is what they say.'

'Jonathon is organizing a press conference, so for anyone who isn't totally ignorant my reputation will be fine. He's getting a friend that works for the ACLU to put pressure on the *Concerned Gazette* and Gein-Brewt to print a retraction of some kind. But even without that the press conference will be enough.'

'You think?'

'I hope, but . . . well . . . you know. It should be enough.'

David listens to Charles's sigh. He says, 'It will, Charles. Don't worry.'

Charles chuckles. 'That's easy for you to say, and it's easier said than done.'

<u>CXXXiX</u>

They gather on the steps — near the flag pole by the pillars — with their backs to the Scioto River; the noise of traffic between is a constant annoyance. There is no representative from *AM Concerned Gazette.*

Standing on the landing around the portable podium are a slew of representatives from the PA State Police; the Columbus, OH, Division of Police's Chief; the city's Mayor; Jonathon Lafete; and Charles Grey.

Introductions are made. The Lieutenant Colonel of the PA State Police renders the official statement :

<u>cxl</u>

'It is unfortunate that we are here today, but we are here for a just and noble cause. Charles Grey *was* a person of interest in the murder of Corey Lafete. Corey Lafete's brother, who is here in support of Mr. Grey, was also — equally — a person of interest in the murder of Corey Lafete. These facts arose out of diligent investigation into the crime. Let me make the following as clear as crystal : neither were responsible for, nor did either have any involvement in, the murder of Corey Lafete. Thank you. We will now take your questions.'

<u>cxli</u>

Following the official statement many questions are asked. And many questions are answered.

<u>cxlii</u>

They are silent that night as they fall asleep, neither of them talking rather indefinitely until fading off to slumber. The silence falls all at once, like the sky dividing like a torn scroll curling up.

Charles is telling David about the press conference; after the story is told, he ruminates:

'What if I wasn't who I am? What if I didn't happen to be best friends with Corey's brother? Who happens to be an attorney with all the connections that he does have? What would be happening to me then?'

<u>cxliii</u>

'I want to thank you all for coming tonight. This is all way too gracious. I couldn't have been luckier than to have worked for such a good and fine company. I couldn't have been luckier than to have worked with so many decent folk. And . . . I couldn't be happier than to be retiring!' At this comment there's some hooting and hollering, general clapping, and a few whistles. She continues, saying, 'So, I want to finish by especially recognizing David Guy, who's taking my place in EAD.' She holds her glass up to him. 'Congratulations, David, and good luck to you!' She downs her champagne.

David raises his glass, saying, 'Thank you, Joyce,' and does the same.

After dinner the formality wanes and the real party starts. David, having watched her swill martinis all night, and himself on his third after dinner cocktail, wonders what Elizabeth Cooper is in such a hurry to tell him. She practically runs across the dance floor, past Martin Grimes waltzing with his wife, glaring at the back of his head until she passes them, and then focuses on David with a toothy shark-like grin until she gets to him.

Elizabeth Cooper asks, 'Don't you think he's the killer?'

David, a glass to his lips and taking a swallow, accidentally breathes some alcohol, which makes him simultaneously choke and laugh out of embarrassment. He recovers quickly and asks her, 'Is who the killer of who?'

'Oh, you know!' she says, and laughs. 'Charles Grey. I know they're saying some serial killer from Pennsylvania did it, but there's a lot of theories that Charles and Jonathon did it together.' She's too drunk to realize that she turns to watch Martin Grimes dancing with his wife as she says this.

David also watches them dance for a moment, before lowering his head and shaking it at the floor.

'Well?' Elizabeth Cooper prods.

The biting sarcasm comes out because of the demon liquor as he says, 'No, Elizabeth, I don't think he killed him, I know he did.' David has to keep from smiling in reaction to the look on her face. 'I dare not leave him because I fear for my life!'

The shock on her face is comical and priceless. It pisses David off.

'My God, Elizabeth! I'm kidding! I mean, how do you think? Oh, wait, I guess you stopped thinking after your second Cosmo!'

Elizabeth's shock has morphed to self righteous disdain, as though she's offended by being spoken to in such a manner. David looks quickly round for a place to set his drink, and she puts out a hand in offer to hold it for him. David takes in her air of being injured but willing to help anyway, and he has the urge to throw the rest of his drink in her face. He hands it to her.

'Goodbye, Elizabeth.' David walks away and leaves the party.

'Have a good evening, David,' she shouts after him. 'Don't worry! I'll let Martin and his wife know you've left.'

CHAPTER TWENTY THREE

FRIDAY, JUNE 23RD, 2000 :
THE 'ACCIDENT'

cxliv

There's a van parked where she usually parks, so she has to pull into the driveway. She doesn't like having to pull into the driveway.

Susan sees a woman talking into a microphone and a man with a camera. The man with the camera is filming the woman with the microphone, using the house as background.

cxlv

'I don't know what else to tell you, Ms. Bachman. The evidence is irrefutable.'

'This is total bullshit!'

'I'm sorry, but this has no bearing on the court's custody decision whatsoever.'

'Is that right?'

'Yes. Nothing can be done.'

'Yeah, well, all I know's there's only one thing worse than a pervert, and that's a serial killer.'

'But, Ms. Bachman, he's no longer a suspect. He never really was.'

'This is pointless! You don't know anything at all! I don't even know why I pay you! Tell me! If you can't get me my son back why do I pay you?'

'Ms. Bachman, please! Calm down. I understand you're upset, but there's no call for hysterics.'

'Oh, screw you,' she says, hanging up the phone.

cxlvi

She blows the horn, and she doesn't realize it ruins the camera's take of the microphone. Susan is a kettle full of water over an inferno, heating up and shaking like her idling SUV.

Inside the house the atmosphere is not much more relaxed, and each individual within defines a metric by which to measure the fact. Normally as sedate as a giant teddy bear, Sarah is perhaps the best metric of them all. The dog is restless and pacing, from the base of the stairs near the front door to below the bay window in the living room. Occasionally, she lets go a short talkative bark, preceded by a barely discernible growl.

'Be a good girl, Sarah,' Davey says more than once, 'lie down and be quiet,' but she does not obey.

cxlvii

She's doing her best to ignore the people tapping on her car window. After she blew the horn the first time the woman with the microphone and the man with the camera walked around the back of the Explorer to take position next to her driver's side door. She lowers the passenger window, blows the horn again, leans over and shouts, 'David!', as though everyone in the house should hear her. Microphone's finger turns into a fist, and — instead of tapping — it bangs on the window. She looks at the woman with the microphone and sees that her mouth is moving. Susan lowers the window and says, 'I have nothing to say to you.'

cxlviii

Charles shouts, 'She's here!' It nearly echoes inside the house. 'Damn them,' he utters, referring to Camera and Microphone. He walks to the kitchen with large strides.

'Let's make sure we've got everything. Okay, Davey?' David is helping Davey into his summer jacket.

'I packed my suitcase, Daddy.' The Snoopy suitcase sitting next to him bulges in funny places, filled to the limit with toys.

Charles walks into the kitchen. 'Is the portable phone upstairs on the charger?'

David looks up at him. 'No. It must be where you left it, Charles.'

'There it is,' Charles says, more to himself than anyone else, and he walks over to pick it up from the counter next to the sink.

They head to the front door in single file — Davey followed by David followed by Charles. Sarah, pacing, realizes they're on their way out, barks at them as they approach, and sits at the door, tail thumping the floor impatiently, waiting to be let out.

<u>cxlix</u>

Susan screams, 'What?!?' at the woman with the microphone.

Microphone has incessantly been asking questions, but now takes a breath. The man with the camera is standing behind her. Susan focuses on the camera and stares at the red LED.

'Ms. Bachman,' says the woman with the microphone, 'I understand that you only have your son for the weekends, but—'

Susan interrupts Microphone, loudly saying, 'For the love of Christ I'm trying to live my life here. Now get the fuck away from me.'

The silent gasp from the woman with the microphone makes the sound of the screen door slapping shut seem louder. Susan looks over to the right, but hears the dog barking right away, before seeing the dog running toward the driveway while David holds the screen out again, allowing Davey to struggle through the doorway carrying his Snoopy suitcase himself. The dog races around the front of the vehicle barking ferociously, and Susan barely hears the woman with the microphone shriek, 'Oh my! Oh my! Stay away, stay away! Oh God help us!'

<u>cl</u>

'Your dog ran outside, Charles,' David shouts over his shoulder at him.

Charles says, 'Am I supposed to walk through you two? Just get him outside already; I'll get *my* dog!'

As soon as he can Charles gets around David and Davey, jogging to the far side of Susan's vehicle. From the sound of Microphone's shrieks, he expects to find Sarah tearing into her flesh with her canines, but she's just watching her and Camera, guarding them, her tail happily wagging. The two are huddled together up against the back half of the Explorer. Occasionally Sarah ferociously barks at them, always eliciting a small shriek of woe from the woman with the microphone.

'This is the fourth time I've told you not to trespass,' says Charles, and Sarah barks again. Her bark is like an exclamation point.

His voice quavering, the man with the camera says, 'You need to control your animal.'

'You need to get off of my property!' Sarah barks again. 'Sarah!' Charles shouts. She turns to look at him with a whine, as though rebuked. 'House.' He points to the front door with the portable phone. 'Now!'

Sarah goes as ordered after giving Microphone and Camera one more look. She slowly walks through the yard with her tail down.

Charles says to Microphone and Camera, 'I'm calling the police.'

<u>cli</u>

David opens the rear passenger door.

Susan whips around to look at them and says, 'This is really a great environment to be raising our son in, David.'

He glances at her and then lifts Davey into his booster, having already put the Snoopy suitcase in the vehicle.

'That's fine, David. Don't say anything.'

Charles is on the phone to 911, standing in front of the SUV with his back to them. The microphone is shoved in through Susan's lowered window and the woman holding it rambles off another ignorant question.

Susan whips her head towards Microphone and shouts, 'You bitch! I told you to get the fuck away from me!'

David, leaning in through the lowered front passenger window, says, 'Susan,' while she's still shouting at Microphone. 'Susan,' he says again.

She looks at him.

'Just put the windows up and go.'

'Fuck you, David,' she says. Via body language, however, she lets him know that she's about to put the windows up.

'I love you, Davey,' he says, 'I'll see you on Sunday,' standing up out of the door and turning to walk back to the house.

Susan pushes the buttons to raise the windows. As the one goes up she shouts out to Microphone: 'Didn't your mother ever tell you to mind your own God damned business?'

<u>clii</u>

Mic conspiratorially says to Cam in a whisper-like voice, 'Get behind her; don't let her leave.'

Unquestioningly dutiful, like a slave or a robot, Cam does as told.

CHAPTER TWENTY FOUR

FRIDAY, JUNE 23RD, 2000 (2) : THE 'ACCIDENT'

<u>cliii</u>

There's a new mood changing silence inside the vehicle now with the windows up. Susan drops the shift into reverse and takes her foot off of the brake. She's just beginning to touch the accelerator when she sees in the rearview mirror that the man with the camera is standing directly behind her on the street. She has to slam the brake, making the vehicle rock, to keep from hitting him.

Except for the very loud hum of the air conditioner, all she hears is the tumultuous turmoil of the voices in her head. *Who do these people think they are?*

She's determined to break free. To not be controlled. Using her mirrors she quickly estimates that she can escape through the yard and over the curb, around the back of *their* van.

Nearly on automatic pilot, Susan throws it into drive, slams its accelerator, and cuts its wheels to the right.

<u>cliv</u>

David is almost back to the front door when he hears it roar.

On the portable phone to 911, Charles turns at the same sound : the growling of a wheeled motorized monster known as a sport utility vehicle.

An uncontrollable, childishly gleeful expression appears on Microphone's face when she realizes what's happening, which instantaneously changes into concern. But Microphone has nothing to worry about, because Camera is recording it all.

Sarah, the dog, is sitting in the middle of the lawn, barking; totally unaware.

It's David who notices that Sarah's sitting in the proposed path of the roaring monster SUV.

<u>clv</u>

He runs at the dog, shouting her name. He hears the roar of the engine stop. He senses something coming. When he thinks about it afterward he remembers seeing it come, if only peripherally.

But then he feels as though he's flying. He never remembers hitting the ground. He only remembers that he comes to lie upon it, as if awakening, and he's aware of excruciating pain. The pain is so that it is a definition; not merely a feeling.

And the dog is still barking.

Otherwise, time and the very rotation of the Earth — everything — stops for a moment, as though some macrocosmic pause button has been pushed.

clvi

In a moment that may be forever she exists only within herself — roiling — externally sitting with hands that are white knuckled fists around the steering wheel and feet depressing the brake with all possible force. She doesn't believe it. She cannot believe what just happened. For Susan the moment ends when Davey, forgotten in the backseat, begins to terribly wail.

'Don't cry, baby,' she says, 'it's okay. Don't be afraid.'

Susan gets out of the vehicle and stumbles towards David.

clvii

There is no such moment for Camera and Microphone. They are unpausable; forever crawling.

The woman with the microphone creeps toward David's broken body, while the man with the camera focuses on the image of Davey, crying alone in the backseat.

clviii

Already on the phone to emergency services, Charles says, 'Oh my God. She just ran him over.'

The 911 operator asks, 'What did you say, sir?'

In a slightly more hysterical manner, Charles says, 'My partner's ex-wife just hit him with her SUV.'

He rushes over to David and is the first to get to

his side.

'Yes!' Charles says, kneeling, 'yes, yes, he's still breathing. He needs an ambulance.'

<u>clix</u>

Focusing only on her want and destination — to hover over David's head — and stumbling toward it, Susan prays:

God, please, don't let me have killed him.

Then she realizes he's alive and thinks:

I should kill him.

She notices Charles's pale face staring at her with a look of horrific disbelief that's whiter than the portable phone he holds up against it.

Susan snarls, 'Get away from my husband.'

He has no semblance of control over reasonable Charles when *you psychotic bitch* blurts out of his mouth. Charles then says, 'That man is not your husband, Susan ... Dear.'

The water in the kettle that is Susan erupts, whistling, and her tears flow freely. 'You ... you, Grey. You're a wannabe. A sad fucking substitute. He will always be my husband.'

<u>clx</u>

Microphone hisses over her shoulder to Camera in an attempt that's anything but clandestine, 'Jimmy! You better be getting this!'

And, just so you know, Sarah is being the good

dog that she is through all of this, having had enough excitement, panting attentively in front of the door.

150

CHAPTER TWENTY FIVE

FRIDAY, JUNE 23RD, 2000 (3) : THE 'ACCIDENT'

clxi

Every teardrop from Susan's face that plummets to the ground at her feet feels like the sting of the scorpion to Charles, as though he's the frog giving it a ride across the endless pond. But, he is not the frog.

Charles unleashes his words, and they attack: 'You fucking cunt don't fuck with me. I have zero sympathy for you. None at all. How dare you stand there and weep! As though you're sorry; you're bullshit. And David hates you! I hate you! Your son will hate you. I'm going to make sure of it.'

'Do *not* speak of my son to me you waste. I will fucking kill you.'

Charles glances at the man with the camera and the woman with the microphone, hating himself that moment for being glad they're there. He says, 'I don't doubt you'd try, Susan Dear. Like you just tried to kill David?'

She spits at David with weepy phlegm, and the spit lands in his hair and on the ground around his head. 'He deserves to die,' she says. 'For taking my son from me, he does.'

Charles hears sirens approaching and knows this is almost over, but he gives her one more push:

'Always your husband and you want him dead! The father of your only child!' Shaking his head as he takes a backward step, Charles points at her with the portable phone in a gesture owning an undeniable power of accusation as he says, 'You really are one twisted bitch.'

Susan is shaking. Her tears taper and she shakes. Tension is building as she says, 'You . . . you . . .,' and then she screams, 'Fucking faggot! Go suck a cock and die!'

David moans. The police arrive, the ambulance arrives, and Susan is arrested while EMS evaluate David's condition.

CHAPTER TWENTY SIX

THE NEXT DAY : SATURDAY

<u>clxii</u>

'I think he's waking . . .'

David feels a hand on his arm and a face near his.

'It's me, David. It's Charles.'

<u>clxiii</u>

David is waking up with difficulty, but he's in a stark hospital room. The smell of coffee is stronger than the typical antiseptic smell of health.

He feels confined. The pain in his leg is a dull thumping sensation. It's in a cast and up in a stirrup. He hears Charles's and others' muffled voices. He tries to open his eyes and focus on them.

The room is too white and the shadows too dark. As David strains for focus the white begins to fade.

clxiv

'He should be totally lucid in about fifteen minutes.' This turns out to be the doctor. 'I'll be back in a few hours.'

'Thank you.' This is Charles.

Eventually he begins blinking again, and the smiling face of Charles materializes in front of his eyes as if floating.

Charles says, 'You should see yourself, David.'

Sounding to himself far away with a dry raspiness he says, 'I can feel it.'

clxv

'Mr. Guy, we need to ask you a few questions about yesterday afternoon.'

David looks but for a moment sees only two tall blobs of blue. He blinks a few times and finally recognizes the police officers. He doesn't mean to ignore them when he looks back to Charles and asks, 'Where's Davey?'

'He's at the house. Missy Dandridge is sitting him.'

David tries to shift himself in the bed, and the pain that courses up from his leg inside the cast — although muted by a medicinal drip — is intense and not yet common. He cringes, and his face seizes. As the pain passes, he sees that Charles, too, is making an empathetic face of discomfort.

David asks, 'How bad is it?'

'Not as bad as it must seem, thankfully—'

Charles is interrupted by the very loud clearing of

Officer Lee Stark's throat. David and Charles both turn their attention to the two police officers.

Trish Hunter steps forward and, as though she's perhaps apologizing for her partner's rudeness, she says, 'I realize you have a lot on your mind right now, but we do only need a few minutes of your time.'

Charles and David both nod, but then an acute pulse of pain originates in David's broken leg. He cringes again. Once it passes he smiles as best he can at Hunter and Stark.

David asks them, 'Are you the only police in the city?'

Trish smiles at his humor, but, gravely, Stark says, 'No.'

The look on David's face quickly becomes humorless.

Stark says, 'We need to hear your version of yesterday's incident,' while pulling out and flipping open his note pad.

clxvi

After he finishes telling the officers what he can remember, David asks, 'Will she be charged?'

'Charges are pending,' answers Stark.

'What will she be charged with?'

'That's the DA's determination.'

'Although,' says Stark, looking to Trish, 'given the history attempted manslaughter is most likely.'

'Why?' asks David, 'I don't think she intended ... ' He shuts himself up, taking in the expressions of the other two men. Slightly defensive, he says, 'I know what she did, but given the circumstances—'

Stark interrupts, saying, 'Before she lawyered up your wife—,' only to be interrupted himself by Hunter.

'Ex-wife, Lee,' she says.

'Excuse me,' says Stark, looking to his partner again, although this time with admonition in his eyes. He says, 'Ms. Bachman claims she was attempting to kill the, er;' he looks though his notepad. He continues, obviously quoting, 'gay fucking dog.'

David doesn't believe it, at least not that she meant it. 'She just said that.'

'Yes, she did,' says Charles, suddenly angry. 'I told you something like this would happen.'

David is shaking his head. 'No, no,' he says, 'it was an accident.'

'For years I've warned you, David. For years! Now look at you! Don't tell me she accidentally ran you over!'

Trying to stay calm so that the pain in his leg doesn't spike, David says, 'I know that woman. No matter what she may say, she did not intend to hit me. Or the dog. She was escaping from those ... those ... those evil media people.'

'That may be, Mr. Guy,' says Officer Stark, 'but statistically domestic disputes such as this only continue to escalate.'

David notices that Trish Hunter nods her head at this and says, *cycle of abuse*, under her breath.

Lee Stark says, 'You should seriously consider purchasing a gun for protection.'

'What was that about?'

'What was what about?' Charles wants an argument. He's been pouting and scowling at David since Hunter and Stark left a few minutes prior.

'Don't, Charles. I'm in too much pain.'

'No, David, don't you!' Although he doesn't understand why, it's clear to David that for Charles the fight is on. 'Don't you lay there like a cripple and make excuses for her! She nearly killed you! She could have killed me!' He pauses for a moment and then adds, 'She could have killed Davey. Whether you know it now or not he's the only true victim here.'

David doesn't know what to say and is afraid he'll say something he regrets if he does speak. Laying there broken, he stares at Charles.

Charles realizes that David is not going to answer him and says, 'What? So I'm the bad guy and she's to be pitied? I don't understand you when you get like this, David. Not at all!' He walks over to a brown paper bag atop a hospital tray table, picks it up, and throws it at David. 'I bought you a bagel. Here, eat it!' he says as it flies.

The bagel bag lands with a soft crumple on the covers covering David's chest.

'Charles!' David shouts after him, 'now, where are you going?'

He stands in the open hospital doorway, and David notices a congregation of nurses and other hospital employees just outside the room. Charles looks back at David just long enough to declare his answer.

'Gun shopping,' he says.

Chapter Twenty Seven

CHRISTMAS

<u>clxviii</u>

The lights are all off except for the tree and a scattering of pine scented candles, and it's peacefully quiet even with soft background music. David sits in a chair, Charles sits on the sofa, and Davey sits on the floor by the tree, because he's going to play Santa Claus. They have a tradition that on Christmas Eve they each open one gift.

Being the youngest, and overwhelmed with the spectacle, excitement and awe — not to mention the sweets — Davey opens his present first. The wrapped box seems bigger than he is, and he stares at it with his hands on top of it for minutes with an indescribable look of anticipatory joy.

David is full of anticipation, too. Davey asked for the toy the previous Spring, but the price tag was too high to warrant it being an everyday gift. In the subsequent months, of course, Davey had seemed to forget he'd wanted it, because he hadn't put it on his Christmas List. So David is anxious to see what his reaction will be.

'Are you going to open it?'

Davey nods, waits another few moments, and then — with a new look — tears into the wrapping paper as though attacking to kill it for food, and failure means starvation. The shredded remains hang off the back of the package as Davey stops to see what it is, and he jumps up and screams in rapturous triumph when he does. He runs then directly to David and throws his arms about him in a huge hug, which surprises David.

Davey releases the bear hug on his father and, resuming his jumping, begins to chant, 'Open it! Open it! Open the box for me, Daddy!'

It's a yellow dump truck.

Charles says, 'I guess that's a success.'

David is still over by the tree, having untangled Davey's truck from all of its packaging. He looks at Charles and says, 'I'll be back.'

He gets into the closet built into the staircase to retrieve Charles's present from the high shelf. As he hands it to him he can tell by his expression that he expects he's being handed what he asked for.

Charles unwraps his gift rapidly, and then he stares at David in bewilderment once he realizes his expectations have been met. Charles is speechless.

Smiling in response to Charles's speechless gratitude, David says, 'Don't shoot your eye out, *Ralphie*.'

<u>clxix</u>

Approximately a score before, they'd had the following conversation :

'I've decided to take Davey to see his mother

over Christmas. Would you prefer Christmas Eve or Christmas Day?'

It is night. David has just gotten into bed, taking the ease of such a thing for granted again too soon after being freed from the crutches. Charles has already been in bed for over an hour, reading.

He lowers the paperback — a true-crime book called *ENGAGEMENT ENVY* by Babbit Coleman — and looks at David over his reading glasses, sitting low on his nose. Charles says, 'Excuse me?'

David ignores his rhetorical tone and says, 'I'm thinking Day would be better, don't you? Since you have that thing in the afternoon with your Aunt.'

Charles just looks at him. Then, dramatically, he looks away to grab his bookmark from the lamp table, inserts it into the book and closes it as though pantomiming, places the book where its mark had been on the lamp table, and, looking back to David after beginning to speak, says, 'First of all, David, I assumed you and Davey were going with me. Second of all,' he pauses and then says, 'why would you even conceive of doing such a thing?'

Now his tone aggravates him, but David swallows down his emotion as best he can. He says, 'Not to argue, but why would we go with you this year when we've never gone before? You're the one who says your Auntie Emma still always asks if you have a girlfriend yet.'

'I want to argue about this, David! You're right, though, about Emma. The old girl is 87. I think her finding out is the only thing that'll kill her; she's only hiding from death with the hope I'll meet a nice girl and carry on the family name. I know how insulting it is, but she's just from a different world.'

'I know you not telling her is out of respect and not cowardice, but come on. Really! When has the world not had gay people? There're gay penguins!'

'Jurassic Park.'

'What?'

'When the dinosaurs ruled the Earth there were no gay people.'

'There were no people of any kind, Charles; besides, the dinosaurs went extinct.'

'Exactly. So will she eventually. She can't live forever even if it feels like it.'

'You'll miss her when she's gone. She's your family.'

'Yes. But so are you and Davey. And I'll only miss the good parts — the good times with her.'

'Don't you see, Charles? That's why I have to take Davey to see his mother.'

'No. It's different. She doesn't deserve it.'

'I'm not doing it for her.'

'I think it's a mistake.'

'Duly noted. But I'm taking my son to see his mother on Christmas.'

'I don't think it's good for Davey. I don't think it's healthy.'

'All he knows is that she's his mother. His mommy. A boy needs his mommy.'

'That woman isn't right, David! She ain't right! Jesus! listen to me! I'm not even speaking English.'

'That's English.'

'*Ain't* is not a word.'

'Ain't it?'

'I'm not in the mood, David.'

'What *ain't* you in the mood for, Charles?'

'God damn you! *Ain't* ain't a word!'

'You said it again.' David smiles. 'If you can say it and everybody knows what you mean then it's a word.'

'Yeah! Well! You know what?'

'No! what?'

'I want that gun!'

clxx

The reception area — the mere fact that there is one — is more spacious and inviting than David had expected.

'I've arranged to visit Susan Bachman.'

'Just a moment, sir.' The man behind the desk turns his attention to the computer screen that's near. After making some interesting facial expressions, he smiles at Davey, then up at David, and says, 'May I see identification, Mr. Guy?'

Thinking about it as he retrieves his driver's license, David says, 'Here,' as he hands it over.

The man barely glances at it and hands it back. He stands, leaning a little over the desk, and points to a set of automatic double doors, saying, 'I apologize; ordinarily you'd be escorted, but we're not fully staffed today. Go through those doors and continue forward until you come to the second set of elevators. The patient is on floor five. When you step out of the elevator go left, then right down the hall. As soon as you make the right you'll see another set of doors. Ring the buzzer that's there and the nurse on duty will get you.'

'So,' says David, 'left off the elevator; then right?'

'Yes, sir.'

'Thanks.'

'Thank you, and you have a Merry Christmas now.'

David gives the man a crooked smile and, raising his eyebrows, says, 'Happy Holidays.' He grabs his boy's hand as he walks away, heading towards the automatic double doors and saying, 'Come on, Davey.'

<u>clxxi</u>

The atmosphere of the place reminds David of a dentist's office. Cool soothing sounds come from hidden speakers in the wall and elevator, but David wonders what uncomfortable and possibly painful procedures are performed behind all of the closed doors, out of sight of scrutiny.

A morbidly obese nurse is waiting for them at the doors to Susan's ward. His age seems late-20s to mid-30s, and he's standing with an extremely impatient look upon his face.

David nods to him and says, 'Hello,' when he sees him.

The fat nurse scowls even more before turning to open the locked doors, which he holds for father and son to pass through in silence. David unconsciously tugs Davey close to him as they approach what he assumes is a nurse's station. There's a female nurse sitting there, watching them approach with a bitterly pinched face, her head moving from short to tall in unabashed appraisal before smiling back at the fat one.

The morbidly obese male nurse hurriedly waddles

past them so he's leading, passing on their right and approaching his colleague with a smirk. 'These are the visitors for room 5315,' he snakes in a jubilant hiss. With an air of leadership and his nose up in the air behind his belly, he walks down the hall of the ward and says, 'This way.'

David pulls Davey closer. Doors to the patients' rooms are unlocked — some are standing open — and there're quite a few of these rooms' occupants ambling about in the hall. Their aimless but constant shuffling is monotonous and unnerving, but they seem to be concerned with only their own thoughts and movements. This fact, and the fact that the fat man is obviously not afraid of them, eases David's instinctual apprehension.

They come to a door with a metal plate to its side that has the numbers 5315 raised upon it, and braille beneath. The nurse has to lift a few folds of his stomach to pull out keys attached to an automatically retracting tether, and he opens the door.

David and Davey enter the room.

Before locking the door behind them the morbidly obese male nurse says, 'I'll come to escort you back to the elevators in an hour.'

clxxii

'Davey! Come give me a hug!'
'Mommy!'

clxxiii

David purveys the room. There's a low cot bed, a bedside shelf bolted to the wall with just a paperback upon it, a bolted rung for hanging garments with attached irremovable hangers — only three with clothes : a repeat of what she's wearing and two with nightclothes — There's a vent at the bottom of one of the walls, and a window opposite the wall with the door. The window is inoperable and has bars on the outside. David doubts that it's even breakable.

clxxiv

The long embrace between Sandy and Davey ends. She holds him out with her hands on his shoulders. She asks him, 'Did Santa get you what you wanted?'

clxxv

David continues to look around. He tries to permit them privacy by memorizing details of her room. He gets lost in his inability to imagine how horrible it must be for her to find herself forced to be where she is.

clxxvi

They talk. Not just mother and son, but the three of them as a family. After many minutes of Susan and

Davey focusing on each other they slowly become a unit again. At least for the latter half of the sixty minutes they have allotted together they do. And the time goes by so fast. Immeasurably fast.

clxxvii

They all know as soon as they hear the sound of the key in the lock. Especially Davey. At the sound, when the adults fall silent, the boy becomes distracted from his play. He looks up into their eyes not with tears, but with something much worse.

'Goodbye, Mommy,' he says, hugging her.

clxxviii

David catches a gleam from his wife's eyes. A gleam he sees only in the eyes of her that he sometimes dreams of. And always to his horror.

The thought just comes : *This is a mistake — Charles was right.*

CHAPTER TWENTY EIGHT

THE LAST DAY (4)

<u>clxxix</u>

David walks back to the kitchen from having turned up the television in the living room. He listens to the local news as he sets the table.

He places plates, water glasses, napkins, forks for him and Davey, chopsticks for Charles, and soy sauce. The task is simple and doesn't take long.

David bends to get a pot out of a cabinet. He gets three mugs out of another cabinet. David walks over to the refrigerator to get the milk, and then he gathers the other ingredients for the cocoa.

<u>clxxx</u>

David makes the cocoa:

He uses the mugs to measure the milk and pours it into the pot. Then he adds a few drops of pure vanilla extract, a pinch of salt, and a dash of cayenne pepper. He measures a spoonful of cocoa and three spoonfuls of sugar into each mug.

David turns on the burner, squatting after he

hears the tiny drumroll humph of the gas igniting to assure himself of the height of the flame.

clxxxi

David walks into the living room during a commercial. He takes a seat to watch the weather, which should be on the news when the commercial ends.

The weather report ends, and David stands, heading to the kitchen to check the milk on the stove. Another wintry gust embraces the house, and his leg aches as he stands. There's a creak from the second floor, but this time David's not certain that it's simply the house still settling.

Listening, staring up at the ceiling — in the direction of Davey's room — where the creak seems to have come from, David's attention is inexorably drawn to the television.

'There was a fire today at the Shady Grove Mental Wellness Institute.'

clxxxii

Princess Artist is reporting the story, and she continues, 'A 911 call reporting smoke at 7:03 this morning did not come quickly enough.'

A full frame live shot of a large building's smoldering remains appears behind her words.

'Witnesses report that the building was engulfed when fire fighters first arrived.'

At the forefront of the steel, wood and concrete ruins is organized chaos. Fire trucks, police lights, stretchers, EMS and patients; the curious, the media, the furious and heartbroken; the helpers and aiders, the lost and confused; the concerned and the opportunistic : all gathered and segregated before the smoke, flames, and ash.

The boxed photograph of a man appears in the upper left of the screen, and the name Michael Robertson appears across the bottom of the box.

Princess Artist's voiceover reporting never stops: 'Michael Robertson — public relations liaison for Shady Grove — has issued a statement that suggests the fire was caused by faulty wiring. We go now live to Fire Chief Joe Benton.'

The photograph disappears and the full screen live shot focuses on the fire chief, who seems to appear out of a flurry of snow. A hand holding a microphone thrusts into the frame, and the chief looks away from the camera. There's soot smeared up the side of his face. Obviously answering an unheard question he says, 'We haven't had time to focus on the cause of the fire. It spread very quickly, though.' He wipes the back of his hand across his brow, tipping back his pristine helmet and smudging his forehead with soot to match his cheek. The helmet doesn't fall off, but a mass of long hair escapes from being tucked up underneath it. 'Right now we're putting out hotspots; waiting for things to cool off so we can begin the search. We did our best of coordinating the evacuation, along with help out away from the building from police and medical. Over a dozen incapacitated patients were rescued. Our hopes are high that casualties will be low, but there's no way right now of knowing who is and who isn't accounted for.'

The smiling face of Princess Artist returns to the screen. 'We have confirmed that two Alzheimer patients who wondered away from the scene in all the confusion were rescued and are back under the proper care. We'll have the latest on this tragedy at 11.'

clxxxiii

David knows. He just feels in his soul Susan is alive; more than that, he knows she escaped. He's certain she is in the house, upstairs in Davey's room.

His mind rapidly flashes recent memory at him : the settling creaks of the house, the pulled out kitchen chair, the unlocked French doors, the light he thought he saw while shoveling snow, the closet . . .

THE CLOSET!

He knows she has a golf club.

BOOK THREE

IV.

Three lives drift on different winds
Two lives ruined
One life spent

AMERICAN TRIANGLE, *elton john*

I lost my love
— my life —
that night.

LAST KISS, *j. frank wilson & the cavaliers*

CHAPTER TWENTY NINE

THE LAST DAY (5)

clxxxiv

'911. What is your emergency?'

'My ex-wife is going to kill me.'

'Excuse me, sir?'

'I have an intruder! Someone broke into my house!' He clearly hears Davey's bedroom door slam; then the adequate amount of silence before the slowly deepening stomp . . . stomp . . . stomp . . . of someone descending the stairs.

It's there then. The fear.

clxxxv

Fear is a web of many things. It is everything that is unknown.

clxxxvi

Sometimes when you become aware of your web it arrives instantly to release you from the terror, and because it comes so quickly you never see it. Sometimes when you are aware, whether you struggle or not, it sneaks up on you, and you don't see it coming. Some other times, aware of the web or not, you never struggle, so it never finds you. Then there are times — like this time — that you see all those eyes and legs approaching to feed; you are trapped, stuck to otiosely struggle and unable to look away, because what you would imagine then would be worse.

<u>clxxxvii</u>

On the phone David is automatically answering questions : name, address, details; and he's listening :

Stomp . . . Stomp . . . Stomp . . . Until it stops.

He creeps to peek down the hallway at the front door, so he can see who's standing there. Edging, edging, and edging out to see, his eyes wide, but there's nothing there except a lit empty hallway.

From the phone, loud enough to be clearly heard in the air about his head: 'Sir? Are you there, Mr. Guy?'

A shadow falls across his back, and he hears — perhaps intuits — a swishing sound through the air. There's a loud struck-crunch.

Susan drives the phone off the wall with the driver. Crouching down, nearly kneeling with his hands going over his head at the same time, and the tension taut on its snakelike cord, David has the phone removed from his grip. He turns around slow and steady, ever the tortoise, once he's over the initial surprise of her golf play.

There stands the once love of his life. She has that

look on her face and a golf club gripped like a sword. She's only slightly disheveled, exasperated with sweat and emotion. 'Don't run,' she says with a voice he's never heard.

David looks to run. He tries to see an escape path without looking away from her. The way down the hall and out the front door is blocked, more from his fear than anything else. The other option is run around the table and through the other rooms. She'll give chase, but maybe she'll be faked out if he makes for the French doors. David takes a small step backward, slightly to the left around the edge of the table.

'Please don't move, David. I've had a long day. I came for my boy.'

David swallows. Felt more in his entire body than just in his throat, the low decibel reverberation is like the downhill gear drop of a diesel engine. He says, 'Davey's not home.'

'No fucking duh, David! Where is he?'

They hear a sound from the stove. Susan isn't aware of cocoa, and so she hesitates. David moves around the table towards the pot, but, slow or not, Susan swings the club over the kitchen table and makes contact with his left shoulder. David goes down, his hands gripping the edge of the sink.

'I have to shut this off,' he says with the strain of adrenalized pain.

Stepping around the edge of the table so that she blocks his easy escape to the dining room, Susan says, 'I don't care. Stand up. Slowly.'

Holding her eyes, he stands up. He tries to say something. 'Susan, I—'

'Shut the fuck up!'

As she screams she wildly swings the club, and David does not miss his opportunity. He dodges and grabs the handle of the pot, burning his index finger on the bare metal, which is hot in its own right but also wet with just scorched and boiling over milk. Susan realizes her miscalculation, and she knows what's coming.

In the first half of a very long second, David musters a force that enters from the ground into his feet and gets to his arms through his torso via his legs. The pot and the white liquid fire inside become an extension of him.

In the second half of that second, Susan drops the golf club and raises up her hands to shield her face. To no avail, however, because the steaming milk cascades horizontally to cover her hair and her face. Her screaming begins immediately.

David watches as the white hot coating transforms her; her mask of fury seems to melt away. For a moment it's the Susan he had long ago fallen in love with, and she's extraordinarily suffering. Her screams turn into siren-like shrieks, and she begins to slowly turn in a circle. Her hands want to touch at her face, but they just hover directly in front of it, twitching and accentuating her shrieks of pain.

Her shrieks quickly begin to pierce directly into his brain like a torturous icepick, and his fear and sense of self-preservation morph into a vengeful rage. He raises the pot high above his head, measuring up the whack, and brings it down onto her head.

She falls, flopping and folding on herself, and ends up lying facedown. Her body is over the golf club, the top half in the dining room and the bottom half in the kitchen.

<u>clxxxviii</u>

David relishes the resultant silence from her screaming. Her breath is short, rough, and labored. Full of hibernation. He stares at her for a few moments, before staring at the white ring left around the inside of the pot. He puts the pot back on the stove and shuts the burner off.

David heads upstairs to get the gun.

Chapter Thirty

THE DAY SHE BECOMES WOMAN

<u>clxxxix</u>

She's asleep and dreaming of her son, of freedom, and of being free to be with her son. She doesn't know how long to the day that she's been incarcerated at the Shady Grove Mental Wellness Institute, but she thinks it's been around seven or eight months.

The first five months, approximately, were endless monotony, like a monopoly game with no monopolies and no end — just around and around and around the board — seemingly forever. Going directly to jail is actually like a reward for her, because otherwise she would move ceaselessly in a circle, having to occasionally contend with an orange or yellow randomness : pay poor tax; pay twice what is owed; pay ten times your roll; even a directive to walk on the Atlantic City boardwalk isn't necessarily a good thing, because somebody else already owns it! The only good things about a game like this are that the bank never runs out of money, and, slowly, over time, everyone playing has more and more money. This latter is, of course, until they start trading.

Christmas is the Great Exception for her. Up until Christmas Day she only feels sorry for herself. After David and Davey visit her, however, she focuses on her son. All of Susan's thought becomes bent upon getting him back.

<u>CXC</u>

She dreams that she's standing in front of a window, looking through bars at the sun. It's impossibly close, and its flickering brightness makes her squint. Then she feels its heat, and she begins to back up from the window. She smells smoke.

<u>cxci</u>

Sleeping, she rolls away from the heat, twisting the covers about her legs. This is uncomfortable, and she begins to wake up. As soon as she realizes that the smoke she smells is a real smell — not just a dream smell — she bolts upright, fully awake, staring at and out her barred window as in the dream just awoke from. She sees flames rising up on the outside, rising like the sun, which is seen at the top of the window due to geography but just above the horizon. The heat from the fire is making the sun shimmer like a desert oasis.

She tries to jump up off the cot and falls, because her blanket is still twisted around her feet. Both of her hands hit the floor as she catches herself; her forehead comes close enough that her short bangs sweep it as she raises her head. As she raises her head, she sees the smoke she has been smelling.

cxcii

The smoke is billowing — thick, nauseous, suffocating : deadly smoke — out of the central air vent in the far corner of the room. There's chaotic noise, which is comprised of many, many voices, shouting, and screams of panic; underneath the whining peal of an emergency alarm and an automated evacuation voice saying, 'This is an exercise. Remain calm and proceed to your designated exit.'

cxciii

She thinks of her skin fusing to metal, like meat sizzling and sticking to a grill.
If it is on the other side of the door I am dead.
She puts the back of a hand to the doorknob. She flinches her hand away, and then she thinks it's cold. She touches the back of her hand to the doorknob again — just to make sure — and again it flinches away. Ultimately : still cold. She grips the doorknob forcefully, and — of course — it is locked.

cxciv

Banging and kicking, she screams, 'I'm in here!'
Over and over she screams, 'I'm in here!'

<h2 style="text-align:center"><u>CXCV</u></h2>

Over and over and over again.

She's locked in a trance, and, 'I'm in here,' is all she says.

<h2 style="text-align:center"><u>CXCVI</u></h2>

A great light shines upon her, and she's flooded with relief like an orgasm. She throws her arms around the man before her — the gentleman with the key — not quite in belief.

<h2 style="text-align:center"><u>CXCVII</u></h2>

She's gripping him as though she's drowning, and she keeps repeating, 'I'm here. I'm here. I'm here.'

With his hands on her forearms, trying to remove them from around his neck, he says, 'We have to get out of here, lady.'

She instantly concurs.

He sees this in her eyes and says, 'I'm searching all these rooms. Just go that way,' pointing.

'I'll help you,' she says.

'Quickly! Take that side!'

She goes, looking into every room along the way to ensure it's empty. All along the way she feels the warmth increasing beneath her feet. The smoke intensifies with every other step. She continues to ignore an ever increasing instinctual alarm to flee.

They reach the main hall of the floor, and there

are people there. They're all patients, either seeming lost or in utter panic, but none of them are going anywhere. An old woman with white wispy hair is just standing and drooling, waiting for the elevator to arrive.

She grabs her. She says, 'They're broken, ma'am. We have to take the stairs.'

'Use the far ones! These are—' He need not say anymore. He's opened the doors to the stairway he's at, and a sooty thickness rolls into the hall. He shouts, 'Don't panic people! Don't get clogged in the door!'

Working together, they coordinate the evacuation of the others. Quickly, they herd the patients through the good door and into the stairwell.

The descent in the stairwell is a nightmare. Around and down along the grey cinderblock walls and down and around the concrete stairs with rectangular landings and metal railings they go, and she never lets go of the old drooling patient woman. All the while they hear voices and terrified screams from above and below. They get caught by and catch up to others descending the stairs, becoming part of an exodus escaping the fire. They can't go down quickly enough, and if one falls, then they will all fall, tumbling down the stairs like a rolling ball of bodies. There's pounding and excruciating cries coming from behind a door at one of the landings. The noise draws their attention to the door, and they slow down as they go past it. Evil tendrils of smoke curl out around the door and get sucked back in with every shrieking beat upon it from the other side. She's able to read the sign beside of it :

2ND FLOOR - SOUTH STAIRWELL
AUTHORIZED PERSONNEL ONLY

'It's no use,' he shouts to her. She looks to him, and he's shaking his head. 'The door is locked at all times. Keep going down!'

CXCVIII

Suddenly, there is light. Light from the sun is streaming in from the open exit door below them.

They emerge from the vertical tunnel on the South lawn of the Shady Grove Mental Wellness Institute. She's out.

She walks several meters and turns to look, hearing the inferno. It's no spot fire and all burning. She turns again and continues to walk away.

'Susan!' It's the young male nurse who'd let her out of her room. He looks at her as she turns around to face him, now relatively far. The controlling look upon his face fades away.

He turns to the nearest group of firefighters he sees and shouts, 'Hey! There's still people in there! Trapped on the second floor! Hey! . . .—'

CXCIX

Her last adventure begins : a trek through Ohioan suburban wilderness. She journeys barefoot through backyards and around dense copses of old forest not yet obliterated by development. In the hour before the snow comes the mushy wet ground gets icy, hardening beneath her feet, and it does not take long for every step to feel as though she's walking on icy spikes.

<u>CC</u>

She sees the fence close through the trees in front of her when she can't feel her feet at all anymore. It's the back of a wooden privacy fence, which she realizes after trying that she can't even kick. Her feet are useless.

Hoping for a loose one, she punches along the vertical planks, until she comes to a hole in the fence. There's a section with several planks missing, and she squeezes through.

She finds herself in somebody's backyard. There's clothesline hung with sheets, frozen in the winter air. The sheets provide good cover for her, though, and she creeps close to the house.

The backside of the house is nearly all glass. There's a small patio with a sliding glass door that opens into a large room. Inside, just on the other side of the sliding door, she spies her prize. There sits a pair of slip-on garden clogs, glittering like gold from the reflection off the glass.

As quick as she can on her miserable feet, she moves from behind the sheet hanging nearest the house and begins to crawl when she reaches the patio. She wraps her hand around the vertical handle of the door and pulls. It begins to move with a soft scraping sound and suddenly stops. She applies more pressure, and the door lifts slightly in its track as it slides open with a loud screech.

She freezes, listening, and she hears footsteps. She reaches out quickly and grabs the clogs.

'Did I hear the back door open?' asks a woman's voice, obviously talking to someone else.

Susan looks to where the voice comes from and sees a hallway opening. That's where the cat appears.

The cat runs in and stops as soon as it can see her, with its tail held high and twitching. The cat grins — like all cats do when prey is within their sight — and meows. The meow is both an accusation and a warning.

The woman's voice, now closer, says, 'Is someone there, Mr. Chester?'

Mr. Chester is eyeing her like a mouse, but she can't move. She crouches with the garden clogs in hand and waits to be caught.

<u>cci</u>

The old woman comes into view. She's large and very old. She's wearing a bright purple kimono with little red-orange dragons — like moths, bees or humming birds — visiting blue, pink and yellow flowers, which are connected by intricate, maze forming, vine-like stems of green with greenish-brown thorns. Her hair is a beehive of red-orange that nearly matches the kimono, her cheeks are dramatically rouged, and her purple eye shadow perfectly matches the purple in her outfit. She looks at Susan, kneeling into her house with her garden clogs in hand, and cocks her head in curious interest.

Susan looks from the old woman down to Mr. Chester after again he meows, and she can't help thinking they look alike.

'Can I help you, dear?' asks the old woman with a smile.

Susan drops the clogs and tries to stand up. Free of any weight for a short period, her feet now refuse to support her. She falls back to her knees, and then totally prostrate in through the sliding door. The warmth hits her, making her dizzy, and she turns her head to face Mr. Chester and the old woman.

The cat floats proudly on its paws over to her and sniffs her nose. He begins to purr and turns around, putting his butt in her face.

'Mr. Chester! Where is your manners? Invite her in before you introduce yourself!'

Susan watches as the old woman steps closer to her.

'Are you alright, dear? Can you get up?'

Susan blows air out of her mouth at Mr. Chester, hoping he'll move his butt away.

'Don't mind him, dear. He's just saying hello.'

<u>ccii</u>

I was eleven when Great Aunt Glilda died at 95. So it can't be her. She can't be here. My God, I haven't thought of her forever.

<u>cciii</u>

'Oh my, Mr. Chester, look at her feet. She be lucky if they ain't got the frost bit. The poor dear.'

<u>cciv</u>

I loved going with Mom to visit her. Her house always smelled of Ivory soap and Roses. She always made hardtack candy. She would always make the cat talk to me, although I know it was a trick. She was squeezing the cat's paw. She didn't have a television, but she had plates and figurines and salt and pepper shakers in every nook and cranny.

'Get out my way, now, Mr. Chester. Momma's gotta help this dear child.'

Am I being lifted? She's too old. Aunt Glilda can't raise me up. I'm far too heavy for her.

Far too heavy.

<u>ccv</u>

'No, dear, that ain't me. Just call me Momma.'

<u>ccvi</u>

Her bed. It's gigantic.

It's so high I can barely get up into it, but it's always so soft, with heavy quilts. The quilts are patchwork — homemade — sewn entirely by hand. I remember Mom told me. Aunt Glilda taught her how to sew when she was a little girl.

But not me.

She was too old to teach me.

<u>CCVII</u>

'What is it, Mr. Chester?'

<u>CCVIII</u>

'Oh, dear. How wonderful! You're awake.'
'How long have I been asleep?'
'Not too long, child. Must be a rush of hurry for you to traipse outside no shoes on them feet. It is winter.'

<u>CCIX</u>

'Drink this tea, dear. It's good for you.'

<u>CCX</u>

Steam rises into her face. She takes the mug.

<u>CCXI</u>

'Momma be right back, dear. I have to put these sheets up.'
The sheets are folded and inside a basket.
'Come with Momma, Mr. Chester,' she says, picking up the basket, walking into another across the current room.

<u>CCXii</u>

Sandy sips at her tea.

<u>CCXiii</u>

'Momma's coming, Mr. Chester.' She emerges from the other room carrying socks and shoes. 'Take these, dear,' she says, handing them to Susan.

'Thank you.' She puts them on. The shoes are a size or two too big, but laced tight they're fine. 'May I use your restroom?'

Susan emerges and says she has to leave, glancing at the garden clogs she had intended to steal.

<u>CCXiv</u>

'I know, dear. You be careful now. And child, Momma loves you.'

She slides the door open saying, 'Thank you, Momma.'

'Anytime, dear. Anytime.'

Susan leaves Momma's house.

<u>CCXV</u>

'Mr. Chester. Ain't no one gonna believe me when I tell 'bout this.'

Chapter Thirty One

SUSAN (I)

CCXVI

She walks down the very center of the street that his house is on. The heavy flurries have covered everything like a thick white blanket, pristine except for her footprints and a single set of tire tracks.

In her scrub-like pajamas, strange socks, and too big shoes, she walks unnoticed in between the tire tracks. It is mid-afternoon. When she turns into his driveway so do the tire tracks, but there's no car there. She smiles with the knowledge that she has arrived.

The front door is locked, so she walks around to the back of the house. The French doors are unlocked, and she pounds the snow from her shoes before entering.

CCXVII

She searches the first floor of the house, opening every door, every drawer, and every cabinet. In the closet under the stairs she finds the golf clubs. She takes one, letting its mitten-like cover fall to the ground.

She climbs the stairs and finds Davey's room. She ponders the story of some of the toys as she looks around his room.

She begins to weep and has to sit down on his small bed. Eventually she lies down and falls asleep.

<u>CCXVIII</u>

Susan. Woman. Mother. I am the cat. The flame. The fury. Hear me roar. I am empty. I am lost. Lost without my child. I don't want to live like this, but how can I change it? What can I do now? Now that it's too late. But is it too late?

It's never too late, because there's always time for now and now is never late. But when is it? How soon is now?

<u>CCXIX</u>

She's running barefoot through the woods. She's not cold although it is freezing. Her hair flows free behind her, and she creates her own wind. She does not run against the wind, because she's running to now.

Far ahead through the trees, through dense undergrowth, stands the child. It is her boy. She runs toward him, not wanting to fail him.

She is closer now, almost there, and she trips. She falls. Beneath her body the undergrowth is.

Hardwood floor. A large stick. Something metal.

Her face hurts. Her hair feels wet.

She plants her hands and pushes herself up. She

stands and hears a noise above her. She looks up.

It's David. He's upstairs.

Susan bends over and picks up the golf club.

CHAPTER THIRTY TWO

DAVID

<u>CCXX</u>

He ascends the stairs two at a time, nearly running to the closet in the master bedroom. Every step being a thought, mood, memory.

He throws open the closet door and falls to his knees before a bolted down safe. He spins in the combination and opens the door to the safe.

He pulls out a loaded clip and the gun. He inserts the clip and chambers the first round. He disengages the safety.

<u>CCXXI</u>

The door to the safe hangs open as David nearly runs back down the hall toward the stairs. He feels safer with the Glock in his hand.

CHAPTER THIRTY THREE

CHARLES (2)

<u>CCXXII</u>

Something queer is in the air. That woman reminds me too much of Susan.

<u>CCXXIII</u>

The snow had stopped for awhile, but now it's again coming down heavily. The falling snow causes an extra glare of headlights, and the slow moving bottleneck of rubberneckers doesn't make it any better. The speed of traffic returns to a bit more normal past the accident, but it's still slow given the dark and the snow.

As they pass the wreck, Charles takes in the muffled beep of a backing up tow truck and the red and blue swirl of police cruiser lights. Davey is sifting through his CD case, occasionally knocking the bag of Chinese food resting on the floor between his feet. Sarah is sleeping as heavily as dogs can in the backseat.

He focuses on the woman who had the wreck. She's standing next to a police officer, and they're watching her car get hoisted up onto the tow truck. The red of her wool pea coat seems an unrealistically bright red every time the red of the police cruiser light spins around. She's wearing old fashioned spectacles that go up like sideways teardrops, giving her a face a feline look, especially under the dark hair that's somehow piled so high on the top of her head.

Charles continuously glances at her in the rearview mirror — for as long as he can see her — once they've passed the accident.

CCXXIV

'You know what, Davey?'
'What?'
'I think we'll be making that snowman tomorrow.'
'Me, too!'

CCXXV

Before they can turn into the driveway, they have to wait for a car coming in the opposite direction to get past them.
There's no need to go that slow.
An older Caprice Classic creeps by them. All Charles can see of the driver is a large pair of ancient hands around, and a brimmed hat that seems to float above, the steering wheel.

CCXXVI

He pulls into the driveway alongside of David's vehicle, wondering why he hadn't pulled it into the garage.

'Let me come around and help you out of the car so that you don't slip. Okay, Davey?'

'Okay, Charles.' Davey is beaming. He'd reached the height and weight requirements to no longer need a booster seat just about a week before, and the act of buckling and unbuckling his seatbelt — once he had mastered it — still indefinably pleases him. It's as though every time he does it the satisfaction is exactly the same as the first time he'd done it.

Walking around to open Davey's door, Charles enjoys the quiet rhythm of the night: the falling snow and the sound of his shoes crushing through the crunchy top layer of it that covers the driveway, leaving white molds of his shoes. He opens the door, picks up the kid, and sets him to stand on the ground.

'Think you can carry the food without falling or dropping it?'

'Of course, Charles. I am so six now.'

Charles doesn't laugh, but he smiles a toothy grin. He says, 'Alright, little man, here you go,' handing the bag of takeout to him. He watches Davey start off toward where the driveway becomes the sidewalk and then opens the back door for Sarah.

CCXXVii

'Come on, girl. We're back home.'

Her eyes open slowly. She lifts her large head and dramatically yawns. Charles knows that she's purposefully taking her time. Suddenly, betraying her size and weight, she leaps from the car, and in graceful bounds frolics over the piles of shoveled snow and into the yard. She barks a short happy bark, lifts her head up to the sky as though she's trying to catch snowflakes on her tongue, and then rolls over and over, messing up the pristine snow of the yard.

He grabs her leash from the backseat and closes the door. He stands there, then, watching Sarah play as Davey makes his way to the front door.

CCXXViii

Davey doesn't want to set down the bag of hexagonal Chinese food boxes and struggles to get the storm door open. He loses his balance but does not fall. He reaches out for the door handle.

CCXXiX

Charles smiles as he watches Davey express such determination, walking down the sidewalk to get into the house encumbered with the large bag of takeout. This is when the sights and sounds of that moment change forever.

CCXXX

He doesn't understand when he hears the approaching siren, nor when he sees the approaching red and blue swirl, reflected ahead of its source by the falling snow. This reflection is ethereal and somewhat familiar. When he sees the police cruiser nearly skid to a halt in front of his house, however, somehow he knows.

He turns to Davey to yell at him to stop and not go into the house, but he doesn't have a chance.

The storm door is resting on the back of his foot. The main door is still swinging open. The boy — as though feeling his gaze — looks at him, smiling with excitement.

Davey gleefully shouts, 'Mommy's here!'

CHAPTER THIRTY FOUR

HUNTER & STARK (2)

<u>CCXXXI</u>

The call comes in from dispatch : a 10-34B. Coincidence or not, they're the closest.

Driving, Officer Hunter says, 'Do you remember that address, Stark?'

'Yep. I certainly do. What do you think about this Hunter? You know the Grove burned down today.'

'I know it did, and I feel like getting there ASAP.'

'Let's hope we're not too late.'

<u>CCXXXII</u>

Hunter smiles. She knows that Stark doesn't have any hope, nor *any* expectations sliding on any scale. Such wonders day in and day out would make it difficult to sleep at night. Good officers quickly learn that the best way to handle the worst of it is to take things as they come; not to ask themselves why people do some of the things they do.

'Dispatch: alpha tango five here en route to 10-34B. Please advise we are running 10-60. Over,' says

Stark into the radio.

'So advised alpha tango five. I'll be here.'

Hunter hits the lights and the siren as she says to Stark, 'I wish these side streets would get plowed.'

Stark nods in agreement.

CHAPTER THIRTY FIVE

SUSAN (2)

<u>CCXXXiii</u>

Her face feels on fire. Melting off.

She imagines cracks crisscrossing across the surface of it, with flapping skin exposing the muscle and blood vessels underneath. She imagines the scalding milk has been acid that ate crevices into her face. The pain pulsates and is more intense in certain places, but it hurts all over.

Holding the golf club so it swings by her side, she walks to a mirror in the living room. She wants to see if her face looks the way that it feels.

She ignores the television.

<u>CCXXXiv</u>

'S!' shouts a hopeful voice.

Pat Sajak says, 'Four S's.'

She doesn't hear the four dings as the blocks light up.

'I'd like to buy an E.'

'Sorry. There are no E's.'

She studies her face in the mirror to the rat-tat-tat of the wheel spinning. It doesn't look anything like she'd imagined, but it doesn't look good, either.

The rat-tat-tat stops with a growing aw of the audience and the tonal fall of the bankrupt consequence. It's the wheel's main misfortune; the only one that's black and white.

Her hair is drying fast, but it's damp and shiny. The most painful patches of scalded skin hurt more and seem to glow redder than red, as though coming alive with anger because she's looking at them.

<h3 style="text-align:center"><u>CCXXXV</u></h3>

She hears David nearly running back down the upstairs hallway. She moves into the arched opening between the living room and the hallway. When she sees his feet descending the stairs she hides herself. She hears muffled footsteps on the round rug just inside the front door at the foot of the stairs. One step, and then a second step she hears on the hardwood floor. The sound of his footsteps stop.

Go, girl. You're on.
Like a batter with one leg attached to a whirligig, she swivels her body out from hiding and into the archway. She swings the golf club — for her son and for her life — with all of her might.

CHAPTER THIRTY SIX

DAVID (2)

<u>CCXXXVI</u>

He stops in front of the arched entryway into the living room. He doesn't see her feet and legs lying on the kitchen floor. That's where they had been. That's where she is supposed to be. And that's where he expects her to be.

He definitely hears the swoosh and peripherally sees something swinging towards his head. He knows that it's the golf club. He looks toward it and uselessly tries to bring his arm up to block it.

The driver strikes his right cheek with such force that it feels like his head explodes. His jaw breaks and a tooth shoots out against the wall, splattering a drizzle of blood across the floor. It leaves a pinpoint of blood where it strikes the wall. The tooth comes to rest in the center of the hallway in front of the closet door.

<u>CCXXXVii</u>

David drops to the floor like a scarecrow released from its post. He badly bruises his tailbone and bites his tongue. Hard. Bringing more blood into his mouth.

Susan moves into the hallway and stands in front of him, and he thinks about shooting her. Her face is horrible, and she's crying. Although it takes her awhile to get the words out, she asks him a question. He's heard the voice asking the question once before. He heard it the first time years ago, in their bedroom, on the day he's since thought of as the day he became man.

She hitches in a sob and asks, 'Why, David ... Gay?'

<u>CCXXXViii</u>

She raises the golf club. He raises the gun and begins to apply pressure to the trigger. She again swings the club, and, as it starts to swoosh down to strike David, they both hear the voice of their son.

'Mommy's here!'

The gunshot rings out like a cannon, and it's nearly deafening in the hallway.

CHAPTER THIRTY SEVEN

CHARLES (3)

<u>CCXXXiX</u>

He hears the unmistakable pop of the Glock from within the house and sees the boy fall. Charles says, 'Oh, my God.'

CHAPTER THIRTY EIGHT

HUNTER & STARK (3)

<u>ccxl</u>

She brings the cruiser to a stop in the least amount of time possible given the weather conditions and the vehicle's engineering. This is why Hunter drives. Stark would have put them into a skid.

<u>ccxli</u>

Forgoing codes, Stark says, 'Alpha tango five shots fired,' into the radio. 'Request backup and medical. Repeat shots fired backup medical requested.'

Hunter is already out of the car, weapon in hand. Her own voice booms inside her head:

'GET THAT DOG UNDER CONTROL.'

She sees that the boy has fallen. His body props open the storm door. She can't let it affect her. Not yet.

She levels her firearm at Susan through the open door.

'SUSAN BACHMAN DROP YOUR WEAPON AND SHOW YOUR HANDS.'

CHAPTER THIRTY NINE

SUSAN (3)

<u>ccxlii</u>

I am Susan. I am Woman. I am Mother. I am Lost.

<u>ccxliii</u>

There must be hope. There must always be. Must be. Hope. Always. Mine.

<u>ccxliv</u>

First things first before the hope he must pay Man will pay I will see to it and never stop until satisfied
And David will die

CHAPTER FOURTY

DAVID (3)

<u>ccxlv</u>

He's lying broken on the floor. He closes his eyes and listens.

<u>ccxlvi</u>

"I SAID TO DROP YOUR WEAPON. I WILL SHOOT.'

'You're nothing to me. Now, David. Absolutely nothing ... absolutely nothing ... absolutely nothing ... absolutely nothing ... absolutely nothing'

Another shot rings out this snowy night. The voices stop.

He hears what must be the driver striking the floor, followed by the sound of her body doing the same.

David passes from consciousness.

CHAPTER FOURTY ONE

CHARLES (4)

<u>ccxlvii</u>

He stands outside in the cold dark, clutching Sarah by her collar to his side. He stands outside of his own house. Watching. And waiting. They're the only things he can do.

<u>ccxlviii</u>

And he cries. Although, the wind of the storm, which whips the flurries into frenzy every so often, makes it difficult to tell. One thing is for certain at the very least, and Charles does not contain his grief just after the thought occurs to him :

I will not be building a snowman tomorrow.

Book Four

V.

The past is never dead. It's not even past.

REQUIEM FOR A NUN, *william faulkner*

Left alone with just a memory
Life seems dead and so unreal.
All that's left is loneliness;
There's nothing left to feel.

YOU DON'T HAVE TO SAY YOU LOVE ME,
dusty springfield

CHAPTER FOURTY TWO

HUNTER & STARK (4)

<u>ccxlix</u>

It always starts simply. Like a blank page or an empty canvas.

Lay in the background first :
A house on a suburban street, which — for all intent and purpose — is no different than houses alongside or across from it up and down the entire stretch of the road. Some of them lack fairytale white picket fences, but there's a public sidewalk and a bicycle lane. The road is lined with streetlamps that know when to turn on and off. Most of the houses have a friendly curved path leading to the front door: an invitation to any passerby to come and knock with no fear of trespass. They all have beautifully manicured lawns, even if there are a few dandelions growing.

Details of time are added :
Write the black of night and the freeze of winter.

The current environment :
Paint the storm of snow.

Then the heartache.

Stark doesn't always understand the senselessness of it all. His grave concern stems from his responsibility to return stability and maintain order. To serve and to protect.

<u>ccl</u>

Officer Lee Stark stands in the midst of ordered chaos : the crime scene : the current tragedy. He watches the bus leave with the dead bodies. He watches the ambulance carry the injured victim to the hospital.

He looks down at where the boy had died, knowing that the thickly congealed and quickly freezing maroon liquid is not a spilled sauce from the plastic bag of Chinese takeout he'd been carrying.

Snowflakes landing on the freezing bloodstain entrance him. A unique ice crystal floats to the surface of the formed cement, and then a change occurs. At first it seems that the snowflake grows larger, somehow becoming a brighter white, absorbing moisture up from the concrete and adding to itself. For a moment its mass and brilliance almost glows as a lone beacon — a star — upon the black maroon sky of the walkway. Next comes the pink, which penetrates from the periphery and bleeds into the center, spreading inward like a moldy growth. Then it becomes red. A red snowflake, glowing in anger like a dying sun. And then it's gone. Gone forever. Eventually leaving only the dark maroon surface it had initially lighted upon.

These changes are stalled in time for him as a single moment : frozen. These moments, frozen, come to him for different reasons, but they come often. He knows that they do not come often enough.

This moment is beauty in stark contrast to terror, but sometimes they come because of awe. When they are awesome, they come for the sake of mere beauty itself. But one came to his partner earlier this evening as they first arrived on the scene. Both were but bare witnesses to death when it set upon her, and during it she was the cause of another ending. Another death. This is the kind of moment that comes all wrong. It's the kind of moment that comes as pure terror. These moments — frozen and terrific — are perhaps the most awful kind.

<u>ccli</u>

Officer Trish Hunter exits the residence and walks to stand by her partner. She asks, 'Are you ready to head out, Stark?'

'Whenever you are, Hunter.'

<u>cclii</u>

Stark studies Hunter's face as she drives on the way back to the station, thinking about the investigation to come. There's always an investigation when an officer takes a life. And Stark knows, this was the first time his partner had ever had to pull her weapon.

'Trish. Do you want to talk about it?'

<u>ccliii</u>

She looks at him. She wants to trust the honest mask of concern upon his face. She wishes to confide in him, but he is colleague before friend.

'Thanks, Lee,' she says, 'but no. Not right now.'

<u>ccliv</u>

He nods at her, trying to understand. He settles back into his seat and stares out of the windshield. Out there, beyond the glass, not in the comfort of the car, the headlights light up the falling snow and the night before them.

At times a whiteout rushes directly to assault the windshield. At other times the snow is at peace and simply falling. It falls in ordered vertical pathways from clouds somewhere high above. Sometimes a strange wind whips it into a sphere or some other familiar shape. Sometimes the shape is non-geometrical. No matter the shape, the strange wind will come and whip it all away in a blink, leaving only the black of night visible. Each snowflake is a dancer, but all perform together in an eternal ballet.

Somewhat perplexed and somewhat relieved, Lee Stark is having a moment, frozen and beautiful.

CHAPTER FOURTY THREE

THE FIRST DAY

cclv

David and Charles — as a couple — don't make it a month after the deaths. In fact — in reality — the breakup takes place the very next day. David's in the hospital, and Charles is there. Visiting.

cclvi

'Is it too much to ask? Is it too much to hope for? All I ever wanted was to be happy,' says David. 'It's the most difficult thing to be happy.'

Charles replies, 'All anyone needs is everybody else.'

cclvii

It's simple, really. It's just too much for David to take. How can Charles argue? What can he say?

'You're too much a constant reminder of it all.'

What could be worse than knowing that it's simply

the mere memory?

215

One Year Later

EPILOGUE

<u>cclviii</u>

It's the first anniversary of the deaths, and David visits both of their graves. He brings nothing to put on Susan's grave.

<u>cclix</u>

He was in the hospital during his son's interment. This fills him with more regret than the guilt-ridden burden of shouldering part of the responsibility for his death. After he was released from the hospital, however, he'd had a dogwood — flowering white — planted above the marker.

<u>cclx</u>

This day is an unseasonably bright warm day, with the promise of Spring in the air. He walks alone and ignores all that surrounds him.

<u>cclxi</u>

He places the yellow dump truck on Davey's grave. It's filled with dirt and winter blooming flowers: holly berry, narcissus and Queen Ann's lace. He places it at the base of the dogwood and laments, weeping. He talks to his son and plays with him. He plays with Davey's toy model of heavy machinery.

<u>cclxii</u>

He remembers a dream on this night. For the first time in a very, very long time — in an almost forgotten it's even possible to remember at all time — a long, long time — David remembers a dream that he dreams.

<u>cclxiii</u>

The dream takes place during a thunderstorm. He's in his first house — the one he owned with Susan — and it's dark.

It's not totally dark outside as the sun is just setting, but with the ominous storm clouds the day seems to already be over.

The lights are out on the inside. David suddenly finds himself in the kitchen with an old fashioned hurricane lamp alight on the table. There's a thunderous knock on the door. It seems to shake the very walls and pounds with a preternatural presence inside of his skull. David does not know who it is.

He's in the wake of a supreme fear : not just

scared but terrorized. He watches himself walk down the stairs with deliberate resistance against his own internal will, but with no obvious success. Then his hand, shaking, is reaching for the door handle.

Slowly, the door swings open with a creak and a flash of lightning. Sonorous rumbling thunder in the aftermath of the lightening, still flashing in the beyond, reveals the cold, wet and pathetic silhouette of a man.

It's neither Davey nor Susan impossibly standing there. Neither of them are moaning boos of blame nor calls for justice with their arms outstretched in horrific need.

His mind sighs with relief. He has nothing to fear because he knows the Man knocking on his door. He has always known Him. He *will always* know Him.

And this Man always knocks. Moment by frozen moment this Man is knocking. Always and forever asking, 'Will you let *Me* in?'

<u>cclxiv</u>

David wakes from this dream all warm shivers. He's wet from sweat, steamy and humid, yet cold under the comforter. He's out of breath, titillated and anxious.

For some reason, giving it no thought, he impulsively reaches for the phone. He calls Charles.

<u>cclxv</u>

David thinks :
Life is too short to wonder. Know.

The End

VI.

www.ingramcontent.com/pod-product-compliance
Lightning Source LLC
Chambersburg PA
CBHW061028100726
47911CB00001B/8